LAST CONTACT

Samuel Best

Get Free SciFi Stories!

DEDICATION

For my nieces and nephews
Wishing you the brightest futures

PROLOGUE

Cold night air chilled Hope to the bone as she stomped through the waist-high grass behind her parents' farmhouse. The grass whispered in a gentle breeze, rippling like the surface of a lake toward the darkness that awaited her. Behind her, the warm glow of kitchen light spilled onto the back porch.

Her evening chores were finished. She had cleaned the dining room table after dinner, washed the dishes, and now it was time to work.

While she was toiling inside, stars had been sprayed across the clear night sky after the last light of the Sun faded behind the western mountains.

Hope repositioned a custom-ordered 120mm telescope on her shoulder and shifted a laptop covered with faded NASA stickers to her other hand. Sharing equal rank with the smattering of NASA logos was a newer Diamond Aerospace sticker, its bright blue chevron swooping like a rocket tail behind white block letters. The laptop's spare battery weighed heavily in her backpack, along with the other gadgets she always brought along for a night of stargazing. As often as she'd complained to her parents about being raised in the middle of nowhere, it turned out to be absolutely perfect for studying the night sky.

She adjusted her thick glasses with a gloved hand and scratched her scalp through a blue wool cap. Long, curly brown locks trailed from beneath the cap, brushing her shoulders.

The grass field behind her parents' farmhouse extended for several acres before it hit the narrow river which marked the edge of the pastures. Hope walked up a low hill and found a folding metal chair waiting for her. It commanded an inspiring view of the river, twinkling with starlight as it meandered by, and of the farmhouse behind her, its small square windows aglow with welcoming light.

Hope set her laptop down on the metal chair and unfolded the sturdy computerized tripod of her telescope.

Her kit came together quickly: battery packs, tracking servos, laser-positioning guides, extra wool blanket, gummy bears. She picked up her laptop and sat in the metal chair, grimacing as the frigid metal bit through her thick pants and padded jacket.

Her body heat warmed it quickly, and she released a captured breath as she draped the blanket over her legs, pulled off her gloves, and opened her laptop.

With a few fast keystrokes, she bypassed several scrolling lines of text—programs compiling in the background for various projects at school—and opened a program called *Hope's Night Sky_V3*. A splash screen of a starscape popped up onscreen with a line of text which read *This program is copyright Hope Avahra, so hands off!*

She paired her telescope's tracking system with her laptop and opened her bag of gummy bears while the servos whirred, automatically moving the scope to where she left off last night. A quick glance at her notebook reminded her she had been focused on galaxy M86 in the Virgo Cluster.

The telescope went still, and a moment later a blurry image materialized on her screen. Hope absentmindedly chewed a gummy bear while her laptop processor crunched the high-resolution image. If she didn't have to spend all of her scholarship money on textbooks, she could get herself a *real* computer, one that could handle more than one image at a time.

She was supposed to have finished with the Virgo Cluster two days ago along with the rest of her classmates so they could move on to quasars, but Hope's program needed to digest more numbers before it spit back accurate distance measurements between galaxy clusters, let alone individual stars. She had reworked the algorithms multiple times, but her results were always off by a significant number of light years.

The entire two-hour lecture on dark matter she sat through at the University of Montana earlier that day had been spent tweaking and updating her algorithms instead of listening. Her digital recorder had captured everything for later review.

As the image on her laptop screen resolved to perfect clarity alongside a steady stream of numbers scrolling upward, she grinned around a mouthful of gummy bears. The myriad galaxies within the cluster took on a sharper appearance as data streamed in.

It was working. Instead of her program telling her that everything in the telescope's field of view was sandwiched on top of each other along one plane, it was, to her surprise, quite accurately predicting the distance between celestial objects along every axis— even objects obscured by something in the foreground.

Hope scribbled a few notes on her pad, still smiling. She glanced back at the screen and her pen froze. Her smile slowly faded as she leaned closer, her pinched face glowing from the light of the screen.

A single red line of text in her program told her there was an unknown object in the sky. Hope zoomed in on that section of the image. Chunky pixels disappeared one by one to be replaced by a crystal-clear region of the Virgo Cluster. In the lower-left corner, a solid black circle with a faint blue corona of light blotted out half of galaxy M87.

Hope dropped her bag of gummy bears into her backpack and sat up. She paused all of her compiling programs and tasked her algorithms with crunching more numbers. The first chunk of data that scrolled up the screen told her the object was nowhere *near* as far away as the Virgo Cluster. Her program placed it a mere four light years away from Earth.

Hope's frown deepened. Surely it was an error in her coding—a glitch in her algorithm. She ran a quick test on the other visible objects in the image and received verifiable data that the program was working without error.

The second piece of data that the distance

program reported was from a celestial mass subroutine she had included in the calculations. Nearly every object she studied in the night sky had already been picked over by countless other astronomers, amateur and professional, yet she liked to verify her own data. Including an extra few hundred lines of code that calculated an object's mass seemed only natural.

Her mass subroutine reported that the solid unknown object was the size of Greenland.

Hope slowly looked at the night sky and pushed her glasses up the bridge of her nose.

Her laptop beeped and her gaze lowered to the screen.

The third bit of data came not from her distance program, but from her trajectory algorithm—a piece of software she'd written that saw infrequent use owing to the fact that she usually studied stationary celestial objects.

It told her the unknown object was moving fast, and it was headed straight for Earth.

1

JEFF

THREE DAYS LATER

Jeff Dolan looked down at Earth from an altitude of 270 miles. He slowly raised one arm of his bulky spacesuit and slid up his sun visor to get an unobstructed view of his little home in the cosmos.

Below, the green and brown mountains and valleys of South America slipped by, giving way to the brilliant blue waters of the South Atlantic.

He and the partially-completed space station behind him orbited the planet at a little over 17,000 miles per hour, bringing him a sunrise every ninety minutes. The next wouldn't be for another thirty minutes. Jeff glanced at his wristpad, checking his remaining oxygen levels. He'd already been outside for two hours, so he'd have to skip the next sunrise.

"All done out here," he said. "Heading to the main airlock."

"Copy that," said Alexandra Dimiov from the station control room. Her calm voice filled his helmet and seemed to linger. In the background, soothing ambient music played over small, tinny speakers. "Thought you fell asleep out there."

"Almost," Jeff admitted, smiling.

He secured his floating tools, reeling them in on their safety cables and stuffing them into the oversized cargo pocket on the left leg of his suit. Next, he unclipped his own tether from a steel hoop on the station's hull and clipped it to the safety line running down the length of the space station from the airlock.

At its current state of construction, the station was a single line of large white boxes intersected by delicate folding solar panel wings. Stuck to one end of the station was a slice of curved metal a quarter-mile long from tip to tapered tip. It looked like a giant orange peel curling away from the station, which was tiny by comparison.

"Everything looking good?" asked Alexandra as Jeff pulled himself along the safety line on the inside of the curved slice of metal, toward the airlock.

"Swapped out the joint servo on arm four again," he replied. "That was our last spare. I'll see if I can repair the damaged one before sending it back with the next resupply."

"Aren't you going home in a week? You can just take it with you."

"I'll check the weight. You know, if the servos keep failing during simple tests, we're going to have more than a few crates of useless equipment back home. We'll need to find a new supplier."

"Kate would just *love* that, wouldn't she?" joked Alexandra.

Jeff chuckled and shook his head inside his helmet. The joint contract the United States government had signed with Diamond Aerospace over the construction of the space station was already over budget, and the station wasn't even ten percent complete. Union negotiations at the company's Mars mining facility had stalled, and hauling materials into orbit from Earth was too cost prohibitive to progress much further. The last thing Kate would want to hear about was added expenses and time delays brought on by simple machine failures.

Jeff floated past a robotic arm folded over on itself like a giant metallic crab claw. He was traversing what would eventually be the inside of a large egg-shaped warehouse in space where the company he worked for, Diamond Aerospace, would build starships. The orange-peel shaped piece of metal was but one slice of many that would come together to form a solid, half-mile long ovoid shell. The robotic arms would line the interior hull of the ovular shipyard.

If everything went according to plan, the launch vehicle under construction in Diamond Aerospace's rocket facility in Cape Canaveral would be the last starship built on Earth, at least by that particular company. Jeff envisioned several shipyards in orbit, available for lease to the government or to private space companies.

He paused and stared beyond the station, into the vastness of space. Only he and a handful of others knew what was out there—knew for certain that humans were not alone in the universe.

A star blinked out of existence in Jeff's periphery, and was shining brightly again half a second later. Humans were not alone in the universe, and the proof was right there, orbiting Earth just far enough away to not be seen from the surface.

The object that blotted out the star was a torus—an alien artifact built by a race that had gone extinct millennia ago due to a cataclysm on their homeworld. Five years past, Jeff witnessed the birth of one of those creatures, brought back from extinction by the machines they had left behind.

Now one of those machines was orbiting Earth, waiting silently...but for what? So far the only impact it had on the human race was to cause a bout of mass hysteria when many of the world governments confirmed it wasn't them who put the giant metal donut in space, and more than a few claimed full responsibility. For the last year, there was no escaping the opinions, speculations, and conspiracy theories surrounding the arrival of the torus. Every other day was predicted to be the end of life on Earth as we knew it.

Yet the world kept spinning, and Jeff kept working.

He continued to pull himself along the safety tether bolted to the hull of the station. Each movement was in slow motion, but he didn't begrudge the deliberate pace. It was a good way to unwind after several hours of work inside the bulky suit.

The alien artifact certainly made him uneasy. He

knew how fast it could travel. It would reach him in a matter of seconds if that was its intent, perhaps even faster. He looked up again, expecting to see another star temporarily blink out as the torus drifted past.

Instead, the ring-shaped artifact was only a few hundred meters away, having moved silently closer. Its matte black exterior absorbed the light of the Sun behind it, creating the perfect silhouette of a donut one hundred meters across. For a brief moment, Jeff could see right through the middle of the torus. Then a shimmer swept across the hole from the inner edge, like a sheet being pulled over a bed, covering the void with a sheet of deeper black.

Jeff's voice caught in his throat as he pulled himself faster along the safety tether attached to the space station. The torus kept pace with the unfinished space station, tracking it in orbit around Earth.

"You alright out there, Dolan?" asked Alexandra from inside the station. "Sounds like you're choking on a cheese puff."

Jeff tapped on his wristpad. "My comm line to the surface is down."

A moment later, Alexandra said, "Mine, too."

"We need to tell them we have company."

"What are you talking about? Sensors aren't picking up anything."

"You won't see it on the sensors. The artifacts don't work like that. Look out the window in Hab-2."

Jeff reached the airlock and keyed in the request for it to open. As he waited, he turned back to look at the torus. It hovered silently, the black sheet that covered its hole staring down at Earth like a malignant eye. It had slipped back from the station, but only slightly, and now it appeared to Jeff as a thin black oval with emptiness inside.

"I still don't see anything," said Alexandra.

A blue light glowed from the center of the torus, reaching out like fingers toward Earth. It crawled over the metal of the space station, bathing it in a vibrant blue light. Jeff instinctively held up his arm to cover his face shield as the light swept over him.

"Do you see it now?" he asked.

Alexandra didn't respond.

"Alex?" said Jeff.

His comms crackled and went silent. The halogen lamps illuminating the half-opened outer airlock hatch flicked off just as the cooling system within Jeff's suit cycled down to a complete stop. His breath was suddenly very loud in his helmet. He tapped his wristpad, but the screen was blank.

"Alex?" he said again.

Jeff mashed the open button for the outer airlock hatch, but nothing happened. He couldn't squeeze his bulky suit through an opening so narrow.

A moment later, the flat hull of the station vibrated like a struck tuning fork. He placed his gloved hand against the metal and the vibration moved into his bones, blurring his vision. The robotic arms bolted to the outside of the hull shook violently, as if they would break free at any second.

Then, suddenly, the vibration stopped.

A comet of blue plasma the size of a skyscraper shot out from the center of the torus. It emerged from the flat sheet of black connecting the inner rim of the artifact.

The comet punched through a white blanket of clouds over South Africa and slammed into the surface of Earth, sending out a shockwave that rippled across the land.

The outer airlock hatch slid open the rest of the way to reveal Alexandra, fully suited, her eyes wide with fear. Jeff's comms crackled to life inside his helmet.

"The station is on emergency backup power," she told him. "My suit power just came back on."

"Did you see it?" Jeff whispered.

Alexandra nodded shakily.

Jeff turned slowly to look at the torus. As silent as a tombstone, it drifted away from Earth, disappearing into the black.

2

KATE

Stacks of binders formed a small city on the floor of Kate Bishop's office. She stood in the middle of the room, hands on her hips, surrounded by paper-filled mini-skyscrapers.

Each binder was a project proposal containing a thousand pages of diagrams, schematics, and safety code.

Kate rubbed her stinging eyes.

She had been steadily moving her company, Diamond Aerospace, away from paper ever since she took over leadership from Noah Bell. It seemed to go without saying that a private space company on the forefront of cutting edge technology would be one-hundred percent digital. Yet the process was not as black-and-white as she had expected. Engineers preferred tangible documents to manipulate. They liked to mark up table-sized blueprints and rip out sheets from their manuals when they were frustrated.

She paid a king's ransom for off-site data storage and processing, yet her office had apparently been deemed a perpetual resting place for every binder on the property.

Her consolation prize was the fact that she was hardly ever in her office. When she wasn't out on the factory floor or flying for business, she was at her beachfront condo, trying not to think about work.

Kate brushed a crumb of her morning danish off her white blouse, and flicked a couple more from the thighs of her gray slacks. Her breakfasts usually consisted of a pastry and a cup of rarely-finished coffee. At about two o'clock she would realize she was hungry and then, more often than not, get so busy that she didn't stop for another meal until dinner.

Except when Jeff was in town. They usually managed to carve out time for a proper lunch together.

A binder atop the nearest stack caught her eye. It was a proposal for something called the Starliner Program. She flipped it open to a random page and scanned the list of construction materials required for this single massive spacecraft.

Her eyebrows went up at the sheer volume of raw ore needed just for the hull. She would have to funnel every ounce of ore coming from the Mars mining facility to the Starliner Program for a decade just to build the shell of one ship.

Yet, scanning the business proposal within the same binder, she was impressed by the projected earnings a single starliner could net the company after two years of operation.

Cruise ships in space, she thought in disbelief. Then she shrugged. *Why not?*

Her phone chimed from somewhere amongst the

miniature city of binders. After the third chime, she found it on the shortest stack, under the paper plate that held most of the crumbs from her pastry.

Her assistant, a young woman named Neesha Jordan, popped up on the screen. She was on the factory floor in the building next door, standing in front of a half-finished tug that was destined for the orbital shipyards. Her black-rimmed glasses reflected the bright rectangle of her own phone.

She tucked a strand of straight, jet-black hair behind her ear and opened her mouth to undoubtedly launch into one of her patented run-on sentences when she suddenly stopped and frowned at Kate.

"You have food in your hair," said Neesha.

Kate swiped at the tips of her shoulder-length brown hair.

"Other side. Just...it's right...you got it."

"What's up?" Kate asked.

"Union shenanigans on Mars is what's up. The rep won't budge until he talks with you."

Kate shook her head. "We've talked a *dozen* times. I don't know what he expects—"

"In person," said Neesha. "He wants to talk in person."

"He's willing to come to Earth?"

Neesha shook her head.

Realization dawned on Kate, and she slowly nodded.

"I see."

"My contact in the union at the mining facility thinks the rep is willing to sign a deal, but he wants corporate to extend the olive branch."

"Extend it halfway across the solar system *in person*," Kate clarified.

"It's only the next planet out, Ms. Bishop," Neesha teased. "Don't be so dramatic."

Kate sighed wearily. "How's it going on the floor?"

Neesha turned her phone to show a wide panorama of the expansive build facility Diamond Aerospace leased from the government at the area known as the Rocketyards in Cape Canaveral. Four small ships were in various stages of construction, along with a larger vessel that was very near to completion.

The founder of the company, Noah Bell, had impressed upon her the necessity of innovation for the sake of innovation, even if there were no immediate tangible benefits for executives' bank accounts. Of course, that was contingent upon money coming in the door elsewhere—hence the government contracts.

Most of the projects on the company's current slate were greenlit under those contracts. Yet the largest ship on the factory floor was commissioned by Kate herself, completely independent of any outside contract—one of those "thirty-for-them, one-for-her" kind of deals.

That ship—the *Luna*—was to be the first of its kind: a modular spacecraft that could be customized for a dozen different purposes. From cargo hauler to research vessel; crew transport to low-orbit permanent space station. Using the standard *Luna* body, modules of varying shapes and sizes could dock with the craft in space.

Kate's design team had done their best to make the *Luna* appear as anything other than a large cube, but, to be fair, there wasn't a whole lot that could be done toward that end short of stripping out vital equipment.

One side of the cube was dedicated to the single-core hybrid antimatter propulsion drive, while the remaining five sides were covered with large airlock hatches. It didn't leave a whole lot of room for aesthetics.

The hundred or so Diamond Aerospace employees on the factory floor crawled over the skeletons of other ships, bolting on bars of carbon alloy in place of bones, adding radiation shielding in place of skin.

"Everything looks good down here," Neesha confirmed, pointing the phone's camera back on herself. "You have that meeting with the Deep Black rep in an hour, then you're scheduled to skip your lunch, as usual, followed by another meeting with the nice lady from the Treasury Department, after which—"

Kate stopped listening when she noticed someone standing at the door to her office. He was a gruff-looking, uniformed military man in his early sixties, with a shock-white buzz-cut and a deep-set frown.

"Neesha, I have to call you back," Kate said, clipping the call. She smiled warmly at the man by her door. "Colonel Brighton. It's good to see you again."

He almost took a step into the office but stopped, casting a quick glance at the stacks of binders.

"Under normal circumstances, I would agree," he replied.

Kate's smile vanished. "Did something happen to Jeff?"

"No," he quickly answered. "Nothing bad. You haven't seen the news?"

Kate laughed without humor. "If only I had the time."

"A meteor just hit South Africa."

"A meteor," she repeated slowly. "I thought the military had a defense system in place for that."

"This one didn't come from deep space," said Brighton. "It popped out of a torus in Earth's orbit, covered in glowing blue plasma."

Kate swallowed hard, trying to process the fact that a torus had been so close to Earth.

"What do you need from me, Colonel?"

"Resources. My hands are tied by six hundred miles of bureaucratic red tape. You could have a team on the ground in South Africa in less than a day, with all the proper permits and liaison credentials."

"Surely you have people already there, at the site."

"I do. But they're not you."

"I'm not a scientist."

Brighton straightened his back. "Ms. Bishop, after all we've been through, I can confidently say you are uniquely qualified to be at ground zero for a situation like this. Dolan is en route back to Canaveral."

"Jeff's coming home early?"

He nodded. "There'll be a private conference where all the details will be laid out. After that, we'll get you and a team of your choice on the first private jet to South Africa." He offered her his version of a smile, which was a slight curling upward at the edges of his lips. "That is, unless you'd rather go to Mars to argue semantics with the union."

"Oh, I imagine that problem will still be there when I get back," she said absentmindedly.

Brighton winked at her. "You never know. I heard a rumor they might be receiving a generous subsidy from Washington...pending an increase in ore shipments, naturally."

Kate smiled, genuinely relieved.

"Well, Colonel," she said. "What's the weather in South Africa like this time of year?"

3

RILEY

Tag Riley—commander of humanity's first mission to Titan—tumbled out of nothingness, fell two meters, and hit the ground. His head cracked against the inside of his helmet, shooting starbursts across his vision.

Breathing hard from the effort, he awkwardly shifted the bulk of his bright orange Constellation-class spacesuit as he rolled over on a patch of damp, spongy, dark green moss.

His view was of a vibrant blue sky streaked by wispy white clouds. Towering trees rose around him, their naked, ash-colored trunks terminating abruptly in three broad branches without leaves.

Nearby was a silver-gray boulder the size of a small car. Next to that, hovering two meters above the ground, was the torus through which he had arrived on this planet.

The hole in its center was three meters across, and the ring of pitch-black material that formed its perimeter was a half-meter in diameter. It floated above him as if waiting for something.

Riley looked around. He was alone.

"Noah!" he shouted.

The nearby silver-gray boulder gleamed from the light of the planet's pale yellow sun. If Riley had landed just a meter to his right, he would have cracked open his face shield. With all he'd been through over the past few days, wouldn't that just be the way to end it? Choking for air on an alien planet.

With a loud groan, he rolled over onto his stomach and pushed himself up to his feet. Mud covered the front of his spacesuit. He smeared some of it across his face shield with a dirty glove, making it only marginally more clear.

He patted the side of his utility belt. Two more flimsy emergency oxygen packs remaining—roughly eight hours of breathable air.

Riley let out a howl of pain as he straightened his back to take in his surroundings.

He was in a sparse forest of those odd, naked trees. Even though they were of slightly different height, they all boasted the same configuration of three broad branches splayed out at their flat tops. The branches bent sharply at ninety degrees halfway to their tips, making the trees look like arms with three-clawed hands grasping for the sky.

In the distance, the silhouette of a jagged mountain range traced an EKG line across the horizon.

Riley jumped in place on the spongy ground and discovered that the gravity was very similar to Earth's own.

He glanced at his wristpad and found that it was caked with dirt. He wiped some away but the screen was blank.

"Bell?" Riley said loudly as he turned to face the hovering torus, his voice loud in his helmet. "Noah!"

He let out a weary sigh and leaned back against the boulder.

This was the third planet he'd visited since parting ways with Jeff Dolan inside the hallway of the torus. He studied the artifact before him now—much smaller than the others he'd seen. Yet he knew that when he went back inside the ring—when he was pulled in through the shadowy door on its black exterior—he would be in a space shared by every torus. The inside hollow of the ring artifact before him now looked barely big enough to crawl through. Yet, once he went inside, the space would prove to be a hallway three or four meters in diameter.

Phosphorescent light glowed under his boots whenever he walked inside that circular hallway. Brilliant aurorae followed his gloved fingertips when he touched the walls.

And there were many doors—doors that led to new worlds humanity did not even know existed.

Tag Riley and Noah Bell had visited two of those worlds together.

The first was a dead planet, seemingly barren of all life. There was no water, no mountains, no structure of any kind—simply a vast landscape of flat ground the color of straw. The sky was a lighter shade of pale yellow, and two suns shone feebly through a gauzy veil, emitting only enough to blanket the world in a melancholy twilight.

Wind tore across the surface, threatening to send Riley and Bell tumbling forever over the unbroken continent if they didn't hold on to each other for support.

The torus they had fallen out of was one of countless others hovering over the ground, spread out toward every horizon as far as the eye could see.

Despite there being no apparent resources to harvest, the tori drew the yellow dust of the planet into the black voids that stretched to fill the inner edges of their rings. Long, narrow streams of swirling dust rose from the ground like devils and tilted into the mouths of the tori.

"Remarkable," Noah said weakly.

Standing next to Riley, he stared at the landscape with unblinking eyes—eyes brimming with tears and filled with wonder.

"We did it, Tag."

Riley looked through the other man's mask. Noah wasn't wearing a protective spacesuit. When they had met inside the torus a few days ago, Noah had just piloted a submarine inside. He was wearing a heavily modified dive suit, with extra layers of protection and increased oxygen capacity—but that was nothing next to the radiation shielding provided by Riley's Constellation-class spacesuit.

Now Noah's face was sunken at his cheeks. Deep purple bags hung under his bloodshot eyes. Riley was sure that if he let go of Noah, he would collapse onto the yellow planet and never get up.

"Let's keep moving," said Riley through his helmet intercom. "We still have more to see."

Holding on to each other, they shuffled against the wind, back to the nearest torus.

"You agreed to come with me," said Noah as they struggled to walk. "Even though you knew it was a one-way trip. Why?"

"Who said it was one-way?"

Noah smiled behind his wide diver's mask. "What's next?"

Riley positioned them both beneath the outer ring of the torus and waited for the shadowy door to slide across the surface of the exterior. The black material soaked in the light around it, making the torus appear to be sheathed in negative light.

"Here it comes," said Riley as the door glided into view.

The vibration started slowly, rattling his entire body. As the door approached, the vibration grew so violent that his vision was merely a blur, with a single black streak through the middle representing the torus.

A few moments later, he and Noah were coughing and sputtering on the hallway floor shared by every torus, having been sucked inside through some mechanism they still couldn't understand.

It took Noah twenty minutes to recover from the physical exertion of that adventure—minutes Riley knew they could never get back. Still, he waited.

They were only on the surface of the next planet for less than twenty seconds.

As soon as they hit the ground after spilling out the side of the torus, Noah began to choke. Without a spacesuit like Riley's, his lungs couldn't handle the vast pressure difference on this strange new world.

The glimpse Riley caught of his surroundings before he carried Noah back to the door of the torus was of blue—just blue, as if they were in the atmosphere of Neptune. He couldn't differentiate between the ground beneath him and the sky above. It was all the same vibrant blue, offering less than a meter of visibility in any direction.

They lay on the floor of the inner torus hallway for a long time after that, Noah's breath coming out in ragged gasps.

From private space entrepreneur to explorer of alien worlds, thought Riley as he waited for Noah to sit up. *Quite the résumé.*

"Let's hope the third one is a little more hospitable," Noah wheezed at last.

And indeed it was.

Riley thought this last planet upon which the torus had dumped him could be a good stand-in for Earth—if it weren't for the fact that he was the only person on it.

After five minutes of solitude, he marched back to stand beneath the torus. He waited for the door to slide across the artifact's void-black surface so he could get back in and look for Noah.

As he was preparing for the transition, Noah blinked into existence at the edge of the torus and fell to the ground with a wet thud. Riley helped him out of the mud and did what he could to wipe some of it off his dive suit.

"There you are," said Riley. "I was starting to think it sent you somewhere else."

Noah groaned and said something from behind his mask but Riley couldn't hear it over the intercom. He tapped the side of his helmet and made a shrugging gesture. Comms were out.

Noah put his hands on his hips and looked around with a huge smile, then promptly undid the slide lock under his chin and popped off his helmet.

Riley screamed at him to put it back on but Noah took a deep breath, coughed once, then laughed.

"You idiot," Riley scolded his friend, knowing he couldn't be heard.

A moment later, he took off his own helmet and hesitantly sniffed the air.

"Smells like wet soil," he said. "And cut grass."

Noah knelt down and, after pulling off his gloves, gently pressed his open palm against the spongy ground. Then he walked to the silver-gray boulder and ran his fingers over its surface.

"This is the place," he said, still smiling.

"Place?" Riley asked, confused. "What place?"

"The place I was hoping to find. The one where...where I..."

Noah's eyes rolled up into his head and he crumpled to the ground.

"Bell!" Riley shouted as he ran to his side.

Riley supported Noah's head and looked around helplessly. Noah's eyelids fluttered open and his gaze solidified.

"Help me over to the tree," he whispered.

Riley supported Noah's weight as they stumbled across the soft ground. He eased Noah down to sit with his back against the smooth, ash-colored trunk. Somehow Noah was looking visibly worse by the minute. His face was a pale green color, and thin lines of blood trickled from his ears.

"Should have...added more radiation shielding to my dive suit," Noah said weakly.

"You don't usually need that sort of thing underwater," Riley replied.

Noah tried to chuckle, but coughed instead.

"At least this is on my own terms." He tapped the side of his head, and Riley knew he was referencing the terminal brain tumor with which he'd been diagnosed.

Riley nodded.

Noah leaned forward suddenly and grabbed Riley's hand with both of his. "We are lucky, Tag. So very lucky." He fell back against the tree and looked up the length of the trunk above him, toward the sky. "No one else has seen this. We've traveled to...other worlds..."

Riley lowered his head as Noah's last breath slowly left his body.

The grave wasn't hard to dig. The soil was loose, and Riley used his hands for most of it. He used a slab of silver-gray rock as a shovel to finish the last half-meter before easing Noah's thin body into the hole.

Next he got to work on the headstone. Using another chunk of rock as a hammer, and one as a chisel, Riley etched the initials *NB* into the slab he had used as a shovel. Then, to the best of his ability, he chiseled a crude rendition of Earth's solar system into the headstone, adding a little arrow pointing toward the third planet from the Sun.

Noah Bell was here, thought Riley as he sank the stone deep into the soft soil. *And this is where he came from.*

Riley set Noah's dive helmet next to the headstone, then he stood up straight and cleared his throat.

"We had some differences," he said. "I can be...bullish, I know. You were stubborn, and driven, and...I...never would have experienced any of these marvelous things if it weren't for you. You gave me a life after I thought I had none." He stood at attention and saluted. "Thank you."

Riley turned and walked away, his jaw set, his eyes hard-focused ahead.

Noah Bell passed away staring up at the sky of an alien planet, which is exactly the way he wanted to go.

We should all be so lucky, thought Riley as he made his way back to the torus.

4

JEFF

Flames engulfed the bell-shaped Cygnus capsule as it plunged into Earth's atmosphere.

The world turned from black to orange through the narrow triangular window of the capsule. Fire licked across the high-temperature quartz glass as if the reentry vehicle were in a stoked furnace.

Jeff was alone in the three-person capsule. He kept his arms crossed over his chest, gripping the straps of his X-shaped harness as his bones rattled. He squeezed his eyes shut as the light outside the window intensified, becoming too bright to observe.

Then the intense orange light vanished, replaced in the blink of an eye with the purest white. Jeff slowly relaxed his body as the vibrations inside the capsule subsided. The reentry vehicle emerged from a solid sheet of cloud above the Atlantic.

Not long after, just as Jeff was getting used to the smooth ride, he was slammed back into his seat as the trio of parachutes in the nose of the vehicle popped free and snapped open. There was one more rough impact as the Cygnus capsule plunged into the calm ocean, followed by a gentle bobbing sensation.

"Canaveral, we have successful splashdown," Jeff said.

"Copy that," came the reply from Mission Control. "Glad to have you back, Jeff. We'll have you out of there in no time."

Jeff unsnapped his safety harness and shifted in his seat in a hopeless attempt to get more comfortable. "No time" by company standards meant he should settle in for awhile.

Two hours later, he stood next to the capsule as it sat dripping on the deck of the retrieval ship. The metal glimmered in the late afternoon sunlight as workers clipped heavy cables to the exterior, securing it to the deck.

The captain stood next to Jeff, observing the action. He wore his military uniform with obvious pride, and had a difficult time concealing his annoyance with the casual attitude the crew often took with their duties. He clenched his jaw as one man paused to light a cigarette after clipping a cable to the outside of the capsule. After a quick wink at Jeff, and while ignoring the captain completely, the worker tightened the cable and went elsewhere on the deck.

Ever since Diamond Aerospace had been taking on more government contracts, more government employees showed up in their day-to-day operations. Jeff stopped asking about it months ago.

"Can you tell me about the comet?" he asked the captain.

"Not for me to say," came the tight-lipped reply.

Jeff nodded as if he'd been expecting such an answer.

"How long until we get back to the Cape?"

The military man checked his watch. "Ten hours for us, two for you."

Jeff's eyebrows went up. "Oh?"

"Helo inbound," he said before walking away.

"Well, how about that?" Jeff muttered to himself as he looked at the Cygnus capsule.

He ran his finger over a black char mark that crawled up one gleaming panel, wondering about Kate. She usually called not long after he returned from the station. He had expected to hear her voice on the other end of the line when he called Mission Control after splashdown.

The concept of "usual" probably doesn't apply given the current circumstances, he mused.

Jeff patted the hull of the capsule and went below deck to get changed.

The next several hours were full of disappointment for him.

Kate wasn't on the helicopter. She wasn't waiting inside the heavily-tinted black security car that picked him up from the helicopter pad at Canaveral Air Force Station, nor was she the first person to greet him inside of Diamond Aerospace's operation center when Jeff stepped into the building with his duffel bag slung over one shoulder, a smile already growing on his face. The smile quickly faded when someone he hadn't seen in months stepped forward and shook his hand.

"Colonel Brighton," Jeff said slowly.

"You weren't expecting me," said the Colonel in his usual gruff manner. "I'd much rather be someplace else, believe me."

The grizzled veteran's uniform was immaculately pressed and his shoes held a mirror shine. If it weren't for the worried look in his eyes, he could have just stepped off the set of a recruitment video.

"Where's Kate?" Jeff asked. "Is she alright?"

"Miss Bishop is fine," the Colonel answered. "She'll be here soon." He paused and glanced at the two aides accompanying him. "There are some things you and I need to discuss before she arrives."

"There's a conference room up on two."

The Colonel nodded and cleared his throat. "Well, then, I'll let you get settled. Meet you there in ten minutes."

He turned on his heels and quickly walked away, his aides close behind. They disappeared into the cafeteria, questions mounting in Jeff's mind by the second.

He kept his head down as he rode the elevator up to the third floor, only offering half smiles and quick nods to those who welcomed him back to Earth. They hurried about on their own missions, seeming every bit as worried as the Colonel.

There would be plenty of time for proper

socialization later, after Jeff had figured out where everything stood with the comet of blue fire he had seen fall from the torus.

His temporary quarters in the operations center consisted of a stiff cot, a writing desk, and a small two drawer dresser that was empty. Jeff dropped his duffel bag on the cot and unzipped it. He pulled out his personal cell phone and cycled through the messages, but found nothing new from Kate.

He decided to change into a fresh t-shirt before the meeting. The one he had worn on the retrieval ship now smelled of salt and diesel. He froze in front of the mirror after he peeled off his shirt, staring down at his chest.

A nasty scar had once covered half his ribcage. On his first journey to Titan, an oxygen compressor exploded right under him, pelting him with shrapnel. Yet now, ever since he mysteriously washed up on the shore of Cocoa Beach after that first ill-fated mission, the scar was gone.

Along with the rest of them, he thought. *All the way back through childhood.*

Indeed, every scar obtained throughout his life had vanished between his first mission to Titan and when he crawled from the ocean near Kate's beachfront condo.

As if the torus knew right where to send me, he thought.

He pulled on a fresh shirt and made his way to the conference room on level two.

Colonel Brighton was already waiting for him

inside, without his aides. He stood with his back to the door, weathered hands clasped behind his back, frowning at a picture of a rocket exploding on the launchpad.

"Never understood why Noah Bell had this framed," he said.

"Maybe it was a reminder that sometimes you have to fail so you can be better prepared for success," Jeff suggested.

"Hmm," said the Colonel thoughtfully. "That's a nice thought." Without looking Jeff in the eye, he turned around and sat in one of the padded chairs that surrounded an oval-shaped table in the middle of the conference room. "You are aware that Bell was diagnosed with a brain tumor not long before the events of your last mission to Titan, are you not?"

Jeff slipped into the chair opposite the Colonel, feeling the obvious shift toward a more official conversation.

"I am aware."

"And what is your opinion regarding the levels of radiation you experienced while inside a torus?"

Jeff had to think about that for a minute. "If I remember my diagnostic readings correctly," he replied, "without the extra layers of protection provided by the Constellation-class space suits, I probably would not have survived long after exposure. Even if I had survived, it would be a miracle to escape without some form of advanced-stage cancer."

Colonel Brighton grunted with approval and nodded slightly as he stared down at the glass surface of the table.

"That is what I suspected," he said, almost to himself.

"Colonel, I beg your pardon, but what does this have to do with the comet?"

The Colonel sighed heavily.

"Within the hour," he said, "this building will be crawling with envoys and officials and policy makers. Much will be discussed, and much will be revealed to you and the other employees at Diamond Aerospace. Thus far, the working arrangement between your company and the government was primarily based on a certain amount of trust. Most of that trust, at least from my end, is a direct result of Ms. Bishop's actions leading up to the...emergence...of the creature from the ocean five years ago. In short, Mr. Dolan, I respect her." He spread out his palms on the glass surface of the table and stared at his hands for a moment before continuing. "While there will be much new information shared during the impending conference, there will also be several gaps, if you catch my meaning."

"You mean they're going to withhold some information," said Jeff with a slight smile. "Nothing new there, Colonel."

"While that is true," said Brighton, "there are two things I think you should know before moving forward. The first is this. The United States Government, along with several other governments around the world, are about to embark on a three-tiered mission to save this planet."

Jeff took a deep breath and let it out slowly. "Is it really that serious?" he asked.

"More than you know," replied the Colonel. "I need to ask you and Kate to step directly into harm's way on this one. You will both be part of extremely dangerous missions from which I cannot promise you will return."

"Well, gee. How can I say no when you put it that way?"

"I'm being serious."

"I'm sure you are," Jeff replied, equally as somber. "I told you after I got back from Titan the last time that it really was the last time. I'm happy to be doing what I'm doing in near-Earth orbit. I don't need to go any farther than that. I made a promise to Kate."

"We all made promises. Unfortunately, promises don't always take world-ending comets into account."

Jeff smiled without humor. "So I'm the bad guy if I say no."

Brighton looked him in the eye. "We all are."

Jeff was silent for a long time. Then he asked, "What's the job?"

"You're to take a ship and rendezvous with a space station in orbit around Venus. You'll assist them with their research of the alien creature."

"Research?"

"I want you to try to talk to it."

Jeff laughed until his eyes watered. He shook his

head in disbelief.

"Is there anyone else who can do it?"

"No one with your unique experience. I don't know if there's a link between the comet and the alien, but the meteor that hit South Africa came out of a torus. That's enough of a connection for me."

"I can't talk to it, Colonel. The only experience I have with it is seeing it rise from the Gulf of Mexico, same as you."

"I have to try everything I can to stop the comet," said Brighton. "We all do."

Jeff shook his head again, stewing. Then he held up a warning finger. "Don't expect me to be happy about it. Kate won't like it, either." He sighed and rubbed his eyes. "What's the second thing you need to tell me?"

"This is highly classified, Dolan. I'm only telling you because I think you deserve to hear it. You can't so much as hint that I told you. If there's a way in the future where you find out a natural way, I'll try my hardest to make that happen."

Jeff studied him a moment. "I can appreciate that, Colonel," he said at last.

"You know the torus was orbiting Earth for almost a year before dropping that comet on us," Brighton continued.

"If not longer. We still don't have sensors that can detect them."

The Colonel nodded. "The comet seems to have the same frustrating characteristic. Even if we had been given more warning, it wouldn't have shown up on any scans. But we'll get to that during the conference." He paused as someone walked past the conference room. Brighton's eyes tracked the person until they disappeared from view, then he pulled out a small tablet from his pocket. "Ever since we learned the torus was up there, we were trying to figure out its purpose. Like you, I assumed that the tori had fulfilled their purpose after bringing their alien creator back to life. And then the critter unceremoniously drifted off into the heavens without so much as a thank you." He swiped at the tablet screen and tapped a long sequence of numbers. "But the comet wasn't the only thing the torus spit out."

He slid the tablet across the table. Jeff scooped it up and pushed play on the video. It was a view of deep space, with hundreds of pinpoint stars in the background.

"The stars aren't twinkling," said Jeff. "Was this taken in orbit?"

"Watch," said the Colonel.

The video zoomed in and settled on a seemingly empty quadrant. A moment later, the torus came into focus.

"I don't see anything."

Jeff held the tablet closer. The view zoomed in farther, but not on the torus itself. It zoomed in on a small figure drifting next to it.

Jeff abruptly sat up straight. "It's a person," he said.

As the figure spun slowly in place, light glinted off the face shield of its helmet.

A moment later, the tablet played a burst of audio static, followed by the gentle breathing of someone wearing a helmet.

"Anyone out there?" asked a familiar voice between breaths. "Sure could use a pickup."

Jeff slowly set the tablet down on the table.

"That's Commander Riley."

"Hellooooo," Riley said in the video. "Anybody home?"

5

KATE

The operations center that housed Mission Control for Diamond Aerospace was a sprawling building of offices and meeting rooms. It was two miles from the Rocketyards, near the launch pads shared with Deep Black and whomever NASA was contracted with at any given time.

Kate rarely ventured beyond Mission Control while in the building. Her company had grown so rapidly after she took over that she now had people working for her whom she'd never met. In the beginning, it was a matter of pride to know them all personally. Now, with her attention stretched between a hundred different projects in three locations on two planets, maintaining that ideal had proven impossible.

Jeff was alone in the conference room when she arrived, dozing in his chair with his feet up on the table.

Kate smiled as she quietly walked over and pinched his nose shut.

He twitched and made a guttural noise deep in his throat. Kate quickly sat down next to him and pretended to read something on her phone right before his eyes popped open.

"I wasn't sleeping," he said drowsily.

"Sure you weren't."

He looked around, bleary-eyed. "Did I miss the meeting?"

She eased from her chair and into his lap.

"Yep," said Kate. "It was a real barn-burner. Brighton said a bunch of mean things about you."

She wrapped her arms around his neck and kissed his cheek.

Jeff frowned. "I knew he'd betray me someday."

He turned his head and their lips met. Kate drew back, staring into his eyes as she cupped his face in her hands. "Now that was very unprofessional."

"I'm just getting started."

His hands found the ticklish spot behind her knees and she yelped laughter as she jumped off his lap.

Colonel Brighton and two aides stopped in their tracks just inside the door, staring.

Kate brushed a strand of hair from her face and cleared her throat.

"Colonel," she said formally as she slid back into her chair.

Jeff reached under the table to squeeze her knee but she slapped him away, suppressing a laugh.

Brighton held up his hands, not wanting to get involved.

41

"Hey, it's not my building."

He sat on the opposite side of the conference table from Kate and Jeff, his two aides beside him. They whispered amongst themselves as they set down several stacks of thin folders on the table, preparing for the meeting.

Apparently, Diamond Aerospace wasn't the only organization who couldn't stop using paper, Kate mused.

She and Jeff held hands under the table while other people gradually filed into the room, taking their seats. Kate didn't recognize any of them. When Brighton asked if they could use the conference room in Diamond Aerospace's operations center, she had expected to see at least a couple of familiar faces.

"Close that door, would you, Tony?" Brighton said to the last person to enter the room. "Okay," he addressed the room. "Let's begin."

His aides stood and handed out thin folders to each of the dozen people seated around the table.

Kate opened hers to see pictures of a large, smoking crater. The surrounding farmland was charred, with deep trenches gouged through the blackened soil. Glowing blue substance covered the site.

"That's the meteor impact crater just below the Namibia border in South Africa," said Colonel Brighton. "It's roughly a hundred feet in diameter."

"There isn't a lot of damage given the size of the crater," said a man next to Kate. He adjusted his glasses and peered closely at the pictures in his folder.

"That's correct," Brighton replied. "There was a core of solid mass at the heart of the meteor, but most of it seems to have been comprised of that blue substance you see in the photographs."

"Who's there now?" asked a man in military uniform next to Brighton.

He was roughly the Colonel's same age, with the same buzz-cut, though his hair was black.

"Stenzik and his team are in charge of the quarantine."

The military man next to Brighton grunted dismissively. "Then expect to hear every detail on the six o'clock news."

"I agree," said Brighton. "That's why we need to move fast. Ms. Bishop and her team will be accompanying me to South Africa as soon as this meeting concludes."

Kate shared a glance with Jeff. The Colonel hadn't mentioned Kate would also be going. Jeff nodded at her slightly, trying to signal that it would be alright. He reached for her hand again under the table.

"Our priority on the ground is to measure any threat posed by the alien substance. A team will remain in Cape Canaveral to determine the origin of the meteor." He gestured toward Jeff. "Jeffrey Dolan will pilot a craft to Venus Lab, where he will attempt to open a line of communication with the creature currently orbiting that planet."

"You can't be serious," said a man to Jeff's right.

"Deadly," Brighton replied, meeting the man's glare. "I am deadly serious, Wallace. That meteor shot out of a torus. The same kind of torus from which that creature emerged in the Gulf of Mexico five years ago. There is clearly a link."

Kate squeezed Jeff's hand under the table. He looked at his lap, ashamed to look her in the eye.

Her heart ached for him. After his return from the second mission to Titan, he had vowed to her that he would never again leave Earth's orbit. Not just for her, but for the both of them. Now he was faced with a difficult choice: break his vow, or do everything he could to help the Colonel.

"Commander Carol Brighton, along with Commander Riley..." said Brighton, pausing while he waited out the surprised murmuring from around the table.

Jeff made eye contact with Kate and nodded slightly.

"Brighton, Riley, and their team will prep a ship named Odyssey to intercept a comet that's going to hit the Earth and cause an Extinction Level Event."

The murmurs exploded into shouting, with everyone trying to be heard at once.

"Have you asked Riley about this?" said Jeff over the din. "What if he says no?"

"He won't," Brighton replied.

The Odyssey, thought Kate. She remembered that ship. It had been one of the first completed vessels under the new government contracts. Diamond Aerospace had little to do with the actual design, though it was built at their facility.

Brighton held up his hands to quiet the room.

"I'll share what I know," he said. "Three days ago, an amateur astronomer in Montana realized that the new star she thought she'd discovered wasn't a star at all. It was a comet headed for Earth."

He took a breath. The room was dead silent.

"My people tell me it's roughly the size of Greenland, and it's speeding up. At its current rate of acceleration, they predict impact in two months."

"Impact with Earth?" someone asked in disbelief.

"That is correct. Now you see why it's imperative we pursue every option to stop that from happening."

"What about the people?" Kate asked. "What will you tell them?"

"Nothing," said Brighton. "There's no time. If we don't figure out a way to stop that comet or alter its course, telling people now won't make one iota of difference."

"It will give them time to say goodbye," Kate said, her voice firm.

That stopped his next thought before he could speak it. He leaned to one of his aides and whispered. The aide nodded and left the room.

"Thank you, Ms. Bishop," said the Colonel sincerely. He addressed the entire group once more, tapping a folder in front of him. "Commander Riley and the crew of the Odyssey will place a fission bomb in the path of the comet to break it apart or knock it off-course. Every government in the world is scrambling to figure out their own game plan. This is ours. We've partnered with more than thirty other countries to pool our resources and information, all with the singular goal of saving humanity."

Jeff pinched Kate's leg to get her attention while the Colonel told an anecdote about his meeting with the President discussing the situation.

He held out his two hands to her, balled into fists. She tapped the left one and he smiled. That hand was empty. Then he opened his right hand to reveal a shining chrome ring, slender and delicate.

Jeff slid the ring onto her left middle finger. It fit perfectly.

"And that's all of it," said Brighton, closing the folder in front of him. He leaned back in his chair, a wave of visible exhaustion washing over him. "I know you can't buy me a lot of time," he continued, looking at each of the attendees in turn. "Whatever you can do to keep your departments in the dark about my departure as long as possible would go a long way to making sure the right people are in control of the situation."

"The right people being you and Ms. Bishop?" asked the military man next to Brighton, his voice thick with skepticism.

Colonel Brighton's exhaustion evaporated. He turned toward the man beside him, barely-contained rage in his eyes.

"The right people being anyone who won't drag their feet or twist this toward their own personal gain for the last two months of human existence. So, in this case, yes, like me and Ms. Bishop."

The military man nodded in deference, conceding the point.

Colonel Brighton stood, and everyone else followed suit.

"Thank you for your time," he said formally. "Ms. Bishop," he added, looking directly at her. "Inform your team that I'll have a car ready to take them to the airport in one hour."

"My team," Kate said, caught off guard. "Right. Okay."

He left the conference room, his aide close behind. One by one the others followed after him, leaving Jeff and Kate alone.

"I felt like I couldn't say no," Jeff told her. "If you think—"

She hugged him tightly, stopping him before he could finish that thought.

"Of course you have to go," she whispered. "But that doesn't mean I have to like it."

Kate sniffed and let go. After a quick swipe at her wet eyes, she held up her left hand, admiring the ring.

"It's chromium," said Jeff. "From one of the Mars shipments. The rest of it went into the Luna. I thought that was meaningful."

"You thought right," she told him.

He held a hand to his ear and pretended he couldn't hear her. "What was that? The part about me being right?"

She hugged him again.

"Don't get used to hearing it," she said quietly.

Kate meant it to tease him, but she couldn't force her voice to be playful. She couldn't help but think about the comet, the crew racing to meet it—and of

Jeff, alone in a ship as it hurtled toward Venus, heading once again away from her and closer to danger.

6

RILEY

Riley sat inside the small conference room, hands folded on the glass table, seething at everyone who walked by without acknowledging him. He wasn't angry because he thought he deserved recognition. He was angry because he had been waiting for two hours without any information as to why he was there in the first place.

After emerging from the torus in high Earth orbit, and after spending two days back on Earth, he had found himself standing in the grocery aisle, basket in hand, staring at twenty different kinds of peanut butter. He had wrongfully shouted at a young employee about why there were so many peanut butter choices, then apologized for his behavior and left empty-handed.

And that pretty much summed up how he felt since his return. Riley couldn't seem to make a decision about anything. The stack of takeout boxes in his hotel room was growing larger with each meal, and he still didn't have a plan about where he was going to live or what he was going to do for work.

When his phone rang in his hotel room later that

night following the peanut butter incident, it could have been his ex-wife asking to go on a date. He would have agreed to it on the spot with zero regrets. Those would have undoubtedly come later. As it happened, it was someone claiming to be from Colonel Brighton's office, asking if Riley wouldn't mind coming in for a debrief. Riley informed the gentleman on the phone that he had already been debriefed forward and backward after he popped out of the torus. But given the circumstances, he would be happy to get out of his self-described casket of a hotel room—even if it meant being scrutinized by more doctors and questioned yet again by government employees with less experience than Riley's little finger.

"Hey!" he barked at a passing government employee.

The young lady smiled and waved at him, but kept walking.

"I'm still waiting!" Riley called after her.

He sank back into his chair, exasperated.

The government mook who picked him up at the hotel drove him to the base at Cape Canaveral in a tinted-out black sedan. Riley hadn't expected to be back there again so soon. He thought maybe Brighton would have moved his operation to D.C. after the second mission to Titan.

A lot had happened after Riley stepped into the torus on Titan while the moon's surface was crumbling around him. For he and Noah Bell, only a few days had passed since they started world-hopping. Yet for everyone back on Earth, five years had gone by.

Riley took the news of his missing five years in stride. What else was he supposed to do? He had seen and heard crazier things on his two trips to Titan. He had gotten a big kick out of the government kid's face when the kid told him about the time difference, and Riley's response was simply, "So?"

The people were still mostly the same, the technology was still mostly the same, and the same type of bureaucrats were still in charge. By Riley's estimation, he considered that a win. Good old stability. That's why he was sitting there in that conference room, steaming about being ignored for two hours—he wanted stability.

"Sorry to keep you waiting," said Colonel Brighton as he hurried into the room and quickly took a seat across the table. He wiped sweat from his brow and smoothed down the front of his uniform.

"It's only time, right?" said Riley.

Brighton grunted. "I have to admit, I missed having your...unique...attitude on the team for the past five years. Too many stuffy bookworms crawling out of universities. Some of them are okay, but..."

He shrugged.

"Why am I here, Colonel?" Riley asked. "I told the shrinks everything I knew. If there's an inch of my body the doctors don't know by heart, I'd be shocked."

Brighton cleared his throat and paused while he framed his thoughts.

"You know about the meteor that hit South Africa

around the same time you returned."

"It's the only thing on the news. No one died, which is something."

"It struck near the border of Namibia. Mostly desert, thankfully. Jeff Dolan was EVA when it passed. Saw it make landfall."

"So he stayed busy. Is he working on the orbital shipyards?"

"Diamond Aerospace is under contract with the government to build six of them, along with a new space station hub. Once this current crisis has passed, I thought about asking if you'd like to be a part of the project."

"I'll check my schedule and get back to you." Riley paused a moment. "Okay, I checked. I'm in."

"I'm sure Ms. Bishop would love to have you on the project. They'll need someone to fly the ships after they build them."

"With all due respect, Colonel, what's the real reason you asked me to come back?"

Brighton tapped on the table while he drew a deep breath.

"There's another one," he said.

"Another one that hit Earth?"

He shook his head. "Another one on the way. Bigger. Much, much bigger."

"Headed here?" Riley asked. "For Earth?"

Brighton nodded.

"When?"

"All we have to go on is a visual image. It doesn't show up on any other sensors, just like the tori. But we've been tracking it, and our best estimates say two months, at most."

"Two months," Riley repeated.

"I'm launching an intercept mission, and I want you to be part of it. If we don't do everything we can to stop that comet before it hits Earth, it will be the end of us."

"You called it a meteor earlier."

"It's a comet when it's in space," said Brighton. "It's a meteor once it hits Earth's atmosphere."

"How can you stop it?" Riley asked.

"With a very big fission bomb. There's all kinds of science involved that I don't have the gray matter to comprehend. The bottom line is that the comet should be mostly energy or plasma, and if we can detonate the right kind of explosive close enough, it should break apart well before it hits our atmosphere. Theoretically."

Riley was silent for a long moment. "You want me to place the bomb."

"I want you to copilot the ship. My daughter is the commander."

"Carol is going?"

"And so is Piper Lereaux."

Riley perked up at that. "Why? She's a linguist."

"Same reason Jeff is going to Venus," said Brighton, "and why I want to send you to the comet. If there's any avenue of communication, I want it open."

"I doubt she can talk to space debris," said Riley. "I doubt I can either, for that matter. I've always been better on the bomb side of things, Colonel. Jeff won't be on the intercept mission?"

Brighton shook his head. "He has a different objective. This is a multi-pronged approach to the same problem, Commander. You're the brute force aspect of the plan."

Riley grinned. "Finally. Something worth coming back for."

7

KATE

The plane jolted, waking Kate from a deep sleep.

"Just a little turbulence," said the pilot over the intercom.

The plane seemed to drop a few feet in the air before leveling out, eliciting gasps from the passengers.

"We're almost through it," added the pilot.

Kate slowly released her white-knuckle grip on the armrests of her chair, trying to relax after several minutes without turbulence. Soon the flight attendants walked the aisles, offering drinks and snacks.

Beside her, Neesha gratefully accepted a cocktail from a young flight attendant and drank it in one quick gulp. The flight attendant looked at her with wide eyes as Neesha gave back the empty cup and gestured with her finger to keep them coming.

"Don't stop now," she said. "Didn't you hear the captain? There was turbulence." As the flight attendant walked away, Neesha added, "Oh, God, I hope those are free."

"Tell the airline to bill you," said Kate, laughing.

"Uh oh. Hysterics setting in?"

"Oh, no," Kate answered sarcastically. "What is there to be hysterical about?"

She sighed and attempted to get more comfortable in her seat, to no avail.

The plane was a Boeing 757, chartered by Colonel Brighton to carry the first round of scientific and military personnel to the meteor impact site in South Africa. It was a mostly-empty flight with only forty people on board.

Kate and Neesha rode with half-a-dozen hand-picked employees from her company. Combined, they possessed enough brainpower to put a dent in any problem they were presented with. Buttressed by the small army Brighton had assured her was on its way to the site, he seemed confident in establishing what he called a "net-positive result for the vast majority of the planet's inhabitants".

"I can't believe you agreed to come," said Neesha after drinking another cocktail.

"Why not?"

"I mean, with all the stuff going on back at the office, and with the Mars union guy giving you the runaround, and with Jeff coming back early, it just seems like—"

"Jeff didn't stick around, either," Kate reminded her.

Neesha studied her boss's face for a moment. "Are you mad about that?"

Kate thought for a long moment. "Not at him. I

can be mad about it and still understand it at the same time."

A big grin spread across Neesha's face. "I love working for you. I really do."

"Do you remember when you first started at Diamond Aerospace four years ago?" asked Kate.

"You mean how my parents kicked me out of the house for not becoming a doctor, and then you hired me, helped me through school, and I went back and showed them my doctorate and it didn't change their opinion of me at all? Is that what you mean?"

"I was thinking more about how everything seemed fresh again. The government contracts were rolling in and new projects were starting every other day."

"Oh," said Neesha. "Right."

Kate gestured around her. "This feels a lot like that."

Neesha thought about it a moment. "Shame about the comet, though."

She gestured to the flight attendant for another drink.

Kate unbuckled her seatbelt and excused herself. She waited out another small jolt of turbulence, then slowly made her way toward the front of the plane and took a seat next to Colonel Brighton, who was watching rain streak sideways on his window.

"Mind if I join you?" she asked.

"Be my guest."

"Colonel, have you ever given any thought to retirement?"

He slowly turned to look at her.

"Is that a joke?" he asked.

She smiled. "No, it's a serious question."

He sighed. "I think about it every day. In fact, I was supposed to be on a beach in Lauderdale this week. These things tend to be put on hold when the world is threatened."

Kate checked her watch: eight hours of flight time down, eight more to go.

"Am I allowed to ask you about the alien?"

He seemed to think about it for a moment. "You can certainly try."

"Where has it been for the last five years?"

"Hugging Venus in low orbit."

"Just sitting there?"

"Just sitting."

"And none of your buddies tried to blow it out of the sky."

He offered a sad smile. "Oh, there was plenty of talk. There was a brief moment three years ago when I thought it might actually happen."

"But you stopped it."

He nodded.

"Do you wish you hadn't?" Kate asked.

Brighton answered carefully. "I don't think destroying the alien would have prevented the meteor. Or the other comet."

"And you sent Jeff so he could talk to it."

"I sent him because we need to pursue every possible way to save our planet. One of the tori brought him back to life. Him and Riley. They have a better chance than anyone of exploiting a link with whatever's out there."

"Exploiting," Kate repeated.

"Poor choice of words," Brighton admitted. "Look, Kate. Venus Lab is safe. It's secure. Jeff is going to see if there's anything he can do to speed up their research. That's all."

"But if the comet hits while he's gone, he'll be stranded on the space station with the others. Stuck in space." She sank back into her seat. "Is he the lucky one, or am I?"

"I think you should revisit the problem in two months. If you still feel bad about it, we'll talk."

"You mean after the comet hits?"

He chuckled, and she couldn't help but join him.

Eight hours later, she was bouncing in the back seat of a Jeep as the driver found every pothole on the way to the impact site.

The roads had been paved for a while before turning into a pitted obstacle course, and the colorful landscape was a welcome change from the storms outside her airplane window. Now, Kate had a hard time seeing anything because of the constant dust kicked up from the road.

Their driver was a stoic man named Farat, who spoke immaculate English and responded to every question as if it were the most serious matter on Earth.

When he had picked Kate and Neesha up from the airport, Kate asked about their luggage.

Farat bowed deeply and dramatically replied, "It will be brought...in another car."

"I think I see it," said Neesha, her voice bouncing along with the Jeep. "There."

She pointed ahead, to a cloud of dust rising from the horizon.

Green farmland stretched around them to both sides, watched over by rocky mountains in the distance. Clusters of low huts punctuated the endless flat expanse.

As the Jeep approached the rising cloud of dust, Farat slowed, driving carefully around potholes that would swallow the vehicle.

"The worst I have ever seen," he intoned.

After another deep bow, he left them at a military checkpoint two hundred meters from the impact site. There were no other structures set up around the crater, just a collection of green military vehicles, and two tanks.

Kate and Neesha showed their photo IDs to the guard at the checkpoint. He scribbled on a clipboard and handed them their security badges.

"Don't lose these," he said. "Anyone caught without them goes to a place they don't want to go. Do you understand?"

They nodded, and he waved them through.

Colonel Brighton met up with them halfway to the crater. He was driving a dirty golf cart with a smeared windshield.

"Need a lift?"

Kate and Neesha climbed in.

"Welcome to your home for the next two months," he said.

Kate looked at the flat landscape. "I hope there's a bathroom."

"It will be a small city by the time we're all set up," the Colonel assured her. Let's take a look at what we're dealing with."

He parked the cart near the edge of the crater. The three of them approached it carefully, peering into the depths of its one-hundred foot diameter.

It wasn't so much a crater as it was a hole punched into the Earth at a near-forty-five degree angle.

"My God," Brighton whispered. "I had no idea it was so deep."

Glowing blue goop plastered the walls of the hole, covering it like webbing. At the bottom of the pit, way, way, down, blue light slowly pulsed.

"We need to block all this off," said Brighton, stepping away from the edge. "Kate, tell your people not to go anywhere near it until we get a system in place."

Blue light pulsed from the depths of the pit.

"I don't think I'll have to tell them twice," she said.

8

JEFF

The spacecraft *Seeker* hummed quietly along as it shot toward Venus.

One of several primary burns from its hybrid antimatter propulsion drive had occurred twelve days ago, just beyond the orbit of Earth's moon. There had been two smaller burns since then, along with a half-dozen minor course corrections from secondary thrusters.

The *Seeker* was roughly a quarter of the size of *Explorer I* and *II*, the ships that had carried Jeff to Titan on his two missions to Saturn's largest moon. It had been constructed without a rotating centrifuge, so there was no artificial gravity for the just-less-than two-week journey to Venus. With such a relatively short trip, there was also no need for a hypergel stasis chamber. Each "night", Jeff slept zipped up in his sleeping bag secured to one side of the cramped crew compartment.

The *Seeker* had been built for speed. To accommodate that notion, it could comfortably carry no more than two crew members in its crew and command compartments. Rations could be added for more, and there was certainly enough space (if only barely), but the oxygen scrubbers couldn't handle that much carbon dioxide.

While the two compartments that comprised the habitable portion of the vessel were diminutive compared to the ships Jeff had a hand in building, little had changed with regard to its propulsion system. The habitable portion of the *Seeker* was a mere seven meters from blunted nose to flared stern, with a single fin protruding from the hull which housed, among other things, the communications equipment.

The ship hauled a twelve-meter-long tube that was three meters in diameter—the antimatter propulsion system. A single bell-shaped engine wash housing protruded from the back of the tube.

Jeff drifted from the crew compartment into the forward command area and strapped into the pilot chair. A control panel of black glass curved around him. Above that was a slender rectangular window, in the dead center of which was the brightly glowing white speck of Venus.

Jeff swiped up on the control panel and waited as the screen populated with the controls for the spacecraft. He called up the design parameters for the propulsion system and swiped quickly through the schematics of its current iteration. His finger paused when he came across the specifications for the solid matter fuel chamber. Someone had tweaked its design so the solid fuel would collect in the chamber nearly two seconds longer before the core spike. Such a pressure variation was well within safety parameters, which meant that the simple two second delay allowed for significantly higher energy output upon fuel annihilation within the chamber.

The result appeared to be a net seven percent gain in efficiency over the original design. He couldn't help but shake his head and smile in appreciation.

At the bottom of the schematic, a small logo for the company Deep Black caught his eye.

Following the dissolution of MarsCorp after Jeff's first mission to Titan, there now only two companies on Earth capable of designing and building spacecraft powered by the hybrid antimatter drive. Diamond Aerospace had survived a near-takeover from the U.S. Government during the events surrounding Jeff's second mission to Titan.

Deep Black had not been so fortunate.

Once the fastest-growing private space company since Noah Bell founded Diamond Aerospace, Deep Black had innovated itself into a financial abyss. Within six months of Jeff's return to Earth, they had liquidated most of their assets and sold the rest to the U.S. Government. The name remained unchanged, but the same could be said for little else.

Even though the ship had been constructed at a Diamond Aerospace facility, the majority of funding had come from Deep Black. Most of Diamond Aerospace's corporate funds were tied up in the Mars mining and orbital shipyard projects.

He ran a quick systems diagnostic and received no errors for his efforts. He settled back into his seat and found a sachet of lemonade in the side pocket of his chair. Jeff drank it thoughtfully as he watched Venus grow ever-so-slightly larger in the window.

With a quick tap of the screen, he sent yet another message to the space station in orbit around the Sun's second planet. He waited a long while, then pulled up another message and sent it back to Earth: Still no response.

Jeff released the empty sachet and watched it spin slowly around the cabin. He wasn't sure what was worse: twiddling his thumbs for two weeks on a voyage to another planet, or sleeping in a hypergel tank and having to cough up that disgusting pinkish gel once he arrived at his destination.

He sighed and reached for the buckle of his safety harness when a yellow box popped up on his console. Jeff tapped the box and it expanded into a video feed. The screen was blank but an undercurrent of audio static crackled over the ship's comm system.

"Identify yourself!" squawked a shrill man.

Jeff blinked in surprise. He tapped the transmit button and said, "This is the Seeker, en route to Venus Lab."

More than a minute later, the static returned. "You! You! Who are *you?!*"

"Um...Jeffrey Dolan. I'm...an engineer. I'm piloting this vessel."

A minute later: "What was your point of origin? And don't say 'Earth'. I want specifics!"

"I launched from Cape Canaveral. It took me

almost two weeks to get this far, and if you don't want company tomorrow, I'll flip this ship around and head home."

The pause this time was longer.

"Okay. You are cleared for approach."

What a relief, Jeff thought.

"But I warn you, for your own safety: we are not alone! See you tomorrow."

The line went dead.

Jeff stared at the blank control console for a long time. Eventually, he unsnapped his safety harness and drifted back to the crew compartment.

He slipped into his sleeping bag and zipped it up to his chin. There wasn't much else he could do before starting the orbital maneuvers around Venus besides rest, and if that peculiar conversation was any indication, Jeff would need as much as he could get.

9

RILEY

Riley sat at the back of the crew cabin of the small shuttle, harnessed between Piper Lereaux and a man named Kenneth Miller. He had introduced himself to Riley as *Sergeant* Kenneth Miller, but didn't elaborate beyond that. He was young, wore the traditional close cropped buzz cut of a military man, and moved with precision, even while wearing a spacesuit. Riley could only guess at his purpose on the mission. Piper didn't seem to know, either. So far, Sergeant Miller was not proving to be the chatty type.

The shuttle had launched from Canaveral mere hours after Riley's meeting with the Colonel. Brighton waived the standard preflight medical checks in favor of a quick launch, stating that if Riley didn't pass the test, he would send him anyway.

Commander Carol Brighton gently guided the shuttle along its trajectory. She sat in the pilot seat, hands hovering above the control panel over her knees.

As the small shuttle circled the Earth, their destination came into view, appearing as a gleam on the dark horizon.

Odyssey had been launched in pieces and constructed in Earth orbit. According to Brighton, it was mostly finished when Diamond Aerospace employees at the Mars mining facility went on strike, halting the arrival of the final materials.

After the first meteor hit, Brighton pulled some strings and called in old favors to get the remaining supplies into orbit. The last bolt had been tightened only two hours before Riley and the rest of the crew were to take command of the ship.

Whereas Diamond Aerospace prioritized function over form out of necessity, resulting in a more industrial aesthetic to their spacecraft, Deep Black's government-approved design of the *Odyssey* seemed as if someone was trying to make a fighter jet in space.

Based on the schematics Riley was shown, they had succeeded.

Its exterior was a smooth shell from nose to stern. Wings served no purpose in space, yet the designer couldn't resist adding two stubby appendages to the midsection of the dart-shaped craft. The cockpit window bulged from the nose like a bubble about to burst. The stern flared over the engine compartment, which housed the powerful hybrid Thermal Antimatter Propulsion System.

All told, the vessel was forty meters in length, with more than half of that dedicated to breathable living space. Without a centrifuge to approximate a semblance of gravity, Riley would be floating free for the journey to rendezvous with the comet headed for Earth.

"Only five days for you and Noah," said Piper with a slight French accent over the intercom of her helmet. "Yet five years for us back on Earth."

"That's the gist of it," Riley replied.

"Tell me, how is that fair? I passed through my early thirties and you stayed...what, sixty-two?"

"I am not a day over my very early fifties," he said defensively.

She laughed easily. "It's remarkable to see you again. I only wish Noah had come back, too."

"He..." said Riley, not quite sure how to finish. "He was happy."

"As we all should be."

"How's Dex?" Riley asked.

Dex Hollander had been an engineer on the second Titan mission. He and Piper were good friends, last time Riley checked.

"Married to a French woman."

Riley gasped in mock surprise. "But not to you?"

Piper laughed again. "Not for lack of trying. We are better as friends. He's teaching in Munich."

"Happy?"

"Very happy."

As the shuttle approached the *Odyssey*, Commander Brighton leaned forward in her seat.

"What on Earth is that?" she asked.

"That wasn't in the designs," said Riley.

The design schematics showed a smooth, rounded nose at the front of the craft—part of the same hull piece that covered the entire ship. Yet an apparatus had been added in front of the cockpit window. A five-meter-square metal platform had been affixed to the nose, perpendicular to the craft. It gave the *Odyssey* the appearance of having its nose glued to a wall. Multi-jointed metal arms folded back onto the craft from the platform, as if the *Odyssey* had hit a robotic octopus at high speed.

"That's new," Sergeant Kenneth Miller said, speaking up for the first time since introducing himself.

"Any idea what it is?" Riley asked.

"Tensor platform," he quickly responded. "The platform contains a steel net that extends beyond the mechanical arms."

"What are the arms for?" asked Piper.

"They're for holding on to whatever's in the net."

"Are they expecting us to catch the comet?" Riley asked.

Carol's hands moved swiftly over the control panel as she started the docking procedure with the *Odyssey*.

"No, they expect us to blow it up. That tensor platform has nothing to do with our mission."

"I think your dad would have at least mentioned it," said Riley.

"That would have made sense," Carol replied. "It's funny what he leaves out sometimes."

She piloted the shuttle to the *Odyssey*'s airlock on the port side. The two ships' on-board systems communicated with each other to align the hatches and extend the docking clamps. There was a gentle bump, then Commander Brighton's control panel pulsed green.

"Good seal," she announced. "Don't take off your suits until we disembark."

Riley slipped out of his safety harness and floated over his seat, one hand barely touching the ceiling to stabilize a slight spin. Piper made her way toward the airlock, followed by Sergeant Miller.

"Hey, what's his deal, anyway?" Riley asked after Miller disappeared. "He doesn't say much."

"He's our bomb tech," Brighton replied.

"We need a guy just for that?"

She shrugged inside her spacesuit. "It's not exactly a pipe bomb, Riley. There are a lot of moving parts, and he knows all of them."

"What about the shuttle?"

"Autopilot back to ISS. Unless you want to skip this journey and fly it back?"

"Not a chance. Speaking of which, why are you out here? I thought the Colonel said something about lockdown if you made it back from Titan. Something about your feet never leaving the planet again."

She spun around in place to look at him. Her platinum pixie haircut was easily visible through her darkened face shield.

"You were on Titan," she said, "so you know what happened to my brother."

"I remember."

"My father knows me, and I know him. We both knew he had to make a show of keeping me Earth-bound for the rest of my career. Who could blame him after losing his son? But we both also knew I couldn't stay there forever." She paused, and her gaze drifted into the distance. "Who could blame me after losing my brother?"

"For what it's worth," Riley offered, "I'm glad you're in charge."

She cocked a half-grin and slapped his shoulder through his spacesuit as she drifted past, toward the airlock.

"The good news is that we get a chance to see how much of your flight training you still remember," she said.

"At least half," he said to her back. "Probably."

Not my fault they wouldn't let me do anything on the last mission, he thought.

Riley hadn't flown since the first trip to Titan, years ago. So much had happened since then that it seemed even longer.

It'll be just like riding a bike, he told himself with muted confidence. *You'll see. Everything's automated anyway, right?*

He gently kicked off from the wall and drifted toward the airlock.

10

JEFF

The *Seeker*'s breaking thrusters began firing twelve hours out from Venus. At that distance, the planet's pale white globe filled the window. A sand-colored patch stretching over the equatorial line turned Venus into a giant eye, impassively watching Jeff's approach.

There was little to do but wait. Jeff made all of his docking preparations, then strapped himself into the pilot seat and passed the remainder of his outbound journey drifting in and out of a light sleep.

When the countdown timer hit twenty minutes, Jeff put on his helmet and slid the neck-lock into place. A burst of cold air hit his cheeks. Several data readouts glowed to life along the upper rim of his inner visor.

The newest version of the Constellation-class spacesuit, the Mark VII, boasted better radiation shielding than its predecessors. It interfaced with a broader spectrum of power packs, each one dependent on the goal of the spacewalk. That flexibility meant one didn't have to carry different suits for different tasks, and turned the suit into a modular system. While its bright orange outer layer would never win a fashion contest, Jeff had grown to like it over the years.

He pulled up the comm interface on the ship's control panel.

"Venus Lab, this is Seeker on approach."

The intercom in Jeff's helmet clicked on.

"Okay," came the raspy response.

"All systems in the green," Jeff continued. "You should be coming into view shortly."

"Fine, fine. Call me if something goes wrong."

The line went silent.

Jeff shook his head. "So much for protocol," he mumbled.

Venus now filled the cockpit window from edge to edge.

"Fifty thousand kilometers," said Jeff. "Starting orbital maneuvers."

He swiped at the control panel and input a sequence of commands. With a few gentle bursts from the orbital thrusters, the ship began a slow spin. The image of Venus slid from the window and was replaced with a panorama of space. A small glint appeared in the distance.

"Venus Lab, I see you. Starting my approach."

The space station orbited Venus at a maximum distance of fifty-five thousand kilometers. Its thirty hour prograde orbit was much faster than the planet's own retrograde spin. Venus was unique among the planets in the solar system. Several moons maintained backward orbits, but Venus was the only primary body to do so.

Jeff let the ship's systems do most of the work. His gloved hands hovered over the control panel. He tapped the occasional acknowledgment box and confirmed the longer thruster burns.

The *Seeker* slowly caught up to the space station.

Venus Lab looked like two identical stations fused together at their noses, creating a mirror image. The design of each half was a rather simple main tube section with four rising solar panels spaced evenly along the outer hull. Each end of the station had a single engine, while several orbital thrusters dotted the exterior. Jutting from the center of the craft, where the two halves met, was a small satellite dish aimed at the surface of the nearby planet.

As Jeff approached, one of the thrusters spat air, sending the station into a gentle spin to better present the *Seeker* with its airlock door.

After an overly cautious dance of alignment, the *Seeker* bumped gently against the station and successfully docked. It kissed Venus Lab at a right angle, protruding from the smaller craft like an elongated tumor.

Jeff pulled himself into the cramped spherical airlock of the *Seeker* and sealed the hatch behind him. After the ready lights flicked from red to green, he cranked the handle on the outer hatch of the station and pushed it open.

No one was there to greet him.

Jeff floated awkwardly for a few moments, waiting.

"Okay," he said to himself finally, then moved into the other ship.

He closed the hatch behind him and pulled off his helmet, drifted into the station's central corridor. It ran the length of the craft save for two small compartments at either end, each with a circular window set into a round door. Several cutouts in the corridor opened onto small workspaces and sleeping nooks.

A man with a mop of dark hair drifted into view behind the window at the end of one of the corridors. He seemed to be using a screwdriver to pry at a cube-like object in his hand. Jeff spun to face him and was about to push himself in that direction when the man's eyes met Jeff's. He drifted toward the window and promptly pulled down a shade to cover it.

"That's Hideo," said a man from behind, startling Jeff. "He's been in there for a week. Won't come out."

The man near Jeff was probably in his early seventies. He wore wireframe spectacles and was bald except for two shock-white tufts of hair behind each temple that stuck out like he'd just licked an electrical socket. Bright green nursing scrubs hung loose on his gaunt frame. Scrawled across the breast pocket in chicken-scratch permanent ink was the name DR. ERIKSON.

"Why won't he come out?" Jeff asked.

Erikson grunted and drifted away down the

corridor. "He thinks I'm trying to kill him."

Jeff stared at the occluded window for a moment longer, then followed after the older man.

"And are you?" asked Jeff.

Erikson grunted again. "Hideo has a flair for the dramatic. If I wanted him dead, he'd be dead!"

"How does he go to the bathroom in that compartment?"

"He sneaks out when he thinks I'm sleeping." Erikson cocked his head toward the sealed compartment and shouted, "But I always know, don't I, Hideo?! *Always!* He sneaks extra rations and he moves my equipment. Petty!"

Jeff blinked. He opened his mouth and shut it several times, then cleared his throat and finally managed to say, "I'm Jeff Dolan."

"I know who you are." Erikson opened a laptop secured to the wall of the corridor and typed rapidly on the keyboard. "Hm. Your ship seems to be in good order. Oh! It has the new 5.0 control operating system! Did you notice any lag after issuing commands?"

"No lag," said Jeff. "You're Niels Erikson, aren't you?"

The older man spun toward him, eyes glaring. "And what of it?!"

Jeff studied his twitching face for a long moment. "The magazine articles described you differently."

Erikson's sneer became a frown, and he turned

back to the laptop. "Yes, well. They got a lot of things wrong, didn't they?"

"How long have you been out here, doctor?"

"Eleven months and thirteen days," he replied quickly. "They were supposed to send a replacement crew. Instead, they sent the news we'll have to stay here another four months, at least. Four months! My poor bones. Sandy was right. She knew, but I didn't listen."

"Who's Sandy?"

Erikson snapped his mouth shut and froze. "It's not important," he said quietly. The tension left his shoulders. "Forgive my lack of manners, Mr. Dolan. We don't have a proper dining area, but I can show you where we keep our stores, if you're hungry."

"What I'd really like is some information."

Erikson slowly closed the laptop, then nodded. "Very well. Let's have a drink, shall we?"

11

RILEY

Riley was alone in the command cabin. He sat in the copilot seat, his attention alternating between the control console in front of him and the view through the cockpit window.

Commander Brighton and Sergeant Miller were asleep in their berths in the crew cabin. Riley and Piper were on duty. She was undoubtedly in the small work lab behind the crew cabin, tinkering with her linguistics equipment. Colonel Brighton had gifted her with an abundance of data the government had collected during crew interactions with the tori, and with the basketball-sized spheres of multicolored light that seemed to power them. Power them, or operate them...no one could decide which was the case.

One of the spheres had communicated with Kate on Earth, according to the report Riley scanned. The Colonel gave Piper every signal that little ball of light emitted in the hope that she could feed it into one of her language processors and discover something useful.

As for Riley, he was content. He was piloting a

spacecraft again, able to reclaim his boyhood dream. *No more peanut butter indecision*, he thought with a smile.

The view out the window was of endless black, save for one small speck of blue in the dead center.

The comet.

The *Odyssey* had passed the Sun at a distance of a hundred million miles four days ago. If the comet's rate of speed remained steady—which, so far, it hadn't—Riley and the others would intercept it in just under two days.

Five weeks to travel from Earth to the Sun and beyond, thought Riley. *Bell designed an amazing engine.*

He thought solemnly about Noah's grave on that unknown planet, and hoped someone would find it someday. Bell was the kind of man to be remembered, he decided.

Riley turned his attention to the command console and swiped through a set of menus to call up the design specifications for the ship. He had gone over them a dozen times since the crew had transferred from their small shuttle to the much roomier *Odyssey*, but he found comfort in memorizing every detail.

The interior of the command cabin was almost spherical, with four chairs aligned two-by-two in the center. The two rearward seats swiveled to access controls built into the flat back wall of the cabin.

Moving aft, one drifted through a narrow tube to enter the crew cabin, where four wall cutouts served as bunks, two to each side. There was a small hygiene station tucked away in a closet on one side.

After that came the work lab and galley, such as it was. A barstool-sized table had been bolted to one wall next to food storage. Everyone ate while they worked and sucked their food through tubes. One of the things Riley had come to admire about his current crew was that they knew they were on a short-term mission and didn't quibble about the details. More people should be like that in a tight spot—willing to give up little luxuries such as tables and chairs for a few weeks.

The work lab was afforded most of the space in that small compartment. It consisted of a proper-sized table and two chairs bolted to the floor beside it. Clamps in the table surface allowed one to secure equipment during experiments or repairs.

A three-meters-long cargo hold behind the work lab section of the ship was accessible only during EVA. It carried the fission bomb the crew was to place directly in the path of the approaching comet.

The rest of the ship was all engine. It had performed three full burns since departing Earth orbit, and a dozen minor course corrections.

Riley glanced out the window once again. The *Odyssey* would have to start its braking maneuvers soon, well before its expected rendezvous with the comet. The ship would have to match its speed heading in the other direction, back toward Earth. That would mean pushing the engine to its limits, as the window for acceleration was much shorter than when departing Earth.

I think I'll run those numbers again, come to mention it, thought Riley.

He called up the burn parameters on the console, but was distracted by a small red rectangle that started rapidly blinking. He tapped it and the rectangle expanded to fill the console.

It was the collision alarm.

Riley tapped again for more details but the alarm vanished.

He squinted through the window, at the tiny blue speck glimmering in the great distance.

The red rectangle flashed again, and this time the ship's intercom let out a shrill *WOOP* of alarm before the console flicked back to green.

Riley quickly swiped over to the ship's sensor logs and navigated to the radar visual. Every scannable wavelength was displayed on that screen. It was blank. He scrolled back through the past minute of data and saw two blips pop up on the screen, each lasting no more than a few milliseconds.

Commander Brighton drifted into the command cabin, still rubbing sleep from her eyes.

"What was that?" she asked groggily.

"Collision alarm," Riley answered. "Two anomalies, but they disappeared."

She peered through the window for a moment, then pulled herself down into the pilot seat and strapped in.

"Send it over?" she asked.

He bundled the data and swiped it over to her side of the console. Soon she was looking at the same thing Riley had pulled up on his side.

"Two warnings," she confirmed. "More than one object each time."

"What?"

She zoomed in on her screen and froze the timeline at the moment the ship's sensors registered the anomaly. At least a dozen green dots glowed on the screen.

"Then they disappear," she said, her brow knit in confusion. "Then come back, then gone again."

"Look," said Riley, nodding toward the window.

"I don't see anything."

"Straight ahead."

Brighton squinted. "It looks like...sparkles. Blue sparkles. What *is* that?"

The console flicked to red.

WOOPWOOPWOOP screeched the collision alarm.

"Suits on NOW!" screamed Commander Brighton into the ship-wide intercom.

The first micrometeor streaked past the *Odyssey* faster than the blink of an eye. It gave only the vaguest hint of blue as it shot past.

Riley unbuckled his harness and launched himself aftward.

"I'll bring yours!" he called back to Brighton.

At the airlock, Piper and Miller floated near each other, bumping elbows and heads while they scrambled to pull on their spacesuits.

"What is it?" Piper asked, her voice nervous.

"Micrometeor shower," Riley answered as he yanked his and Brighton's suits off their wall clips. "Suit up and strap in."

He shoved two helmets toward the front of the ship and floated after them. Brighton was out of her chair waiting when he returned. She snatched up her suit and quickly slipped into it, fumbling with the neck seal.

"Here," said Riley.

He dropped a helmet over her head and slid her neck seal into place. She moved to help him with the same but he waved her off.

"I got it!"

She didn't argue. Instead, she strapped into her chair and opened a data stream back home. As Riley got into his seat beside her, she issued a command for the ship's computer to recommend an evasive course.

It spit back a litany of options, then retracted every one of them.

"It can't lock onto the projectiles!" Riley shouted.

Blue streaks shot past the cockpit window.

Then came the first impact.

TINK!

Riley and Brighton shared a glance. Behind them, Piper and Miller buckled their harnesses.

"What was that?!" asked Piper.

"That was a micrometeor puncturing our hull," said Riley.

TINK-TINK!

The cabin went dark. Red emergency lights glowed from recessed lighting in the wall. The control console was almost completely red.

After a long period of silence, Piper asked, "Is it over?"

No one seemed willing to issue a definitive answer on the subject.

Riley and Brighton cycled through the various warnings on the console, dismissing the innocuous.

"We're venting 0-2," said Riley.

His screen showed a flashing icon of the oxygen pump located just aft of the crew cabin, starboard side.

"I *told* them those wings were *USELESS!*" Commander Brighton growled as she fumbled with her safety harness.

"I'll check it out," said Sergeant Miller.

He unbuckled his harness and floated out of the command cabin.

"Can we plug the leak from here?" Riley asked.

Brighton tapped quickly through a series of warning screens. "Doesn't look like it. Hull's compromised. Pressure is dropping. Slowly, but it's dropping." She looked at him." We have to stop the ship early for repairs."

Riley nodded. "Then let's make it happen."

12

JEFF

Jeff drank his second sachet of lemonade and belched politely, then ate a protein bar and stuffed the wrapper into a trash pocket secured to the wall. He floated in a coffin-sized cutout along the main corridor. Erikson floated in a seated position in the cutout across from him, chugging amber liquid from a large plastic bag through a straw. A small glob of the liquid popped free of the straw and floated into the middle of the corridor. Both men watched it intently.

"How long until we're in visual range of the creature?" Jeff asked.

"Seven hours," Erikson replied. "We'll maintain visual contact for six hours after that."

"It's really not orbiting the planet?"

Erikson slowly shook his head, his eyes glazed and distant. "It is stationary."

"How long has this research station been here?"

"Four years."

"That long?" Jeff said in disbelief.

"They put it here as soon as they discovered

where the alien went after it left Earth."

"How did they keep it a secret?"

"They told everyone it was the Venera-D mission."

Jeff frowned. "I thought that launched over a decade ago."

"And the satellite in orbit around Venus disappeared five years ago, along with the Japanese Akatsuki."

"Do you think the creature destroyed the satellites?"

Erikson shrugged and stretched out in the sleeping compartment. His drink sachet floated away while he zipped himself into the secured sleeping bag.

"Why would it do that but leave us alone?" Erikson pondered. "One more mystery."

There was a loud clank from somewhere in the station and Erikson's eyes popped open wide.

Jeff poked his head out into the corridor just as Hideo slid up the shade over his window. The noise had come from the opposite end of the station.

"That wasn't Hideo," said Jeff.

Hideo snapped the shade back down.

"Just another mystery," Erikson replied. "We have a ghost. Did I tell you this already?"

"No," said Jeff hesitantly. "Well, you said you weren't alone. I thought you meant the alien."

Erikson chuckled. It didn't suit him.

"I know how it sounds. I, a man of science, believe this station is haunted by a ghost. Laughable. Absurd!" His chuckle cut off abruptly. "But it's true." He turned in his sleeping bag until his back was to Jeff. "Three weeks ago, it started."

"That's when you stopped sending long-range messages back to Earth."

"That's no coincidence. Our long-range relay was damaged. Sabotaged."

"By...the ghost?"

Erikson sighed. "It doesn't matter. You're here now, and you're going to fix all our problems, yes? You'll understand soon, when we reach the other side."

His words trailed off into mumbles, then transitioned to quiet snoring. Jeff watched the bag of amber liquid spin slowly in the corridor.

A hollow metal clunk came from one end of the station. Jeff looked out of his sleeping compartment as the door swung open to reveal Hideo. He wore gray slacks and a sweat-stained blue sweatshirt. His face was smudged with dirt and his feet were bare.

He motioned for Jeff to join him.

"Is he asleep?" Hideo asked as Jeff drifted into the compartment.

"I'm pretty sure he's drunk."

They were in a storage room of sorts, with supplies strapped to the walls of the spherical space with elastic bands. Hideo had fashioned himself a small workstation consisting of a storage crate atop long cardboard tubes for table legs.

"I am Hideo Tanaka."

He extended his hand, and Jeff shook it. Hideo was about the same age as Jeff, early forties, though the exhaustion Hideo couldn't hide aged him a few years more.

"Do you really think he's trying to kill you?" Jeff asked.

Hideo's eyes darted out to the corridor, where Erikson was sleeping.

"On an emotional level, no. But I must explain what I've seen."

Jeff chuckled nervously. "I have to be honest. This isn't what I was expecting."

Hideo looked at him severely. "Neither were we." He nodded toward an open laptop on his makeshift workstation. "Come. See for yourself."

Jeff grabbed a handhold on the wall and positioned himself next to Hideo, in front of the laptop. Hideo typed quickly, pulling up a data file packed with long lines of text.

"What do you know about our work here?" Hideo asked.

"Nothing. They only told me I would be more help here than back on Earth."

Hideo nodded. "So we start from the beginning. The three of us have been working in twelve-month shifts since the station arrived at Venus."

"Three of you?"

"Listen closely," said Hideo. "Our primary mission is to figure out the alien's purpose for being here. Why Venus? But it has never responded to any external stimuli, nor has it attempted to communicate with us. We were stumped. Sandra figured out a way to retrofit our dish to send controlled bursts of varying wavelengths every time the station passed the alien."

"Sandy," Jeff said quietly.

"We thought that if we ran the whole spectrum, eventually we'd get a reaction." He typed at the keyboard and a line of text was highlighted in bright red. "And we did."

Jeff leaned in to get a closer look.

"Each string here represents a compressed data dump from the station's sensors. Sandra was working alone that night. I was asleep in this compartment with the door open, as was my habit. Dr. Erikson was preparing for sleep when I closed my eyes." He paused and frowned. "There is no way to know what happened between Sandra and Erikson after I fell asleep. What I do know is that Sandra saw something in the data we hadn't seen before. It was the closest thing to a reaction we had received from the alien. A simple, narrow-band wavelength it seemed to be broadcasting into space. Later that night, someone opened the airlock without authorization, and Sandra was gone when I awoke."

"Gone? You don't think she went out the airlock..."

"Dr. Erikson was asleep in his compartment when I discovered Sandra was missing."

"Could she have gone outside without telling anyone and had some kind of accident? Snapped her safety tether?"

Hideo swallowed hard and looked down at his hands. "Her suit is not missing. She went outside without it." The words hung in the air for several long moments. "Sandra...was not suicidal."

"That doesn't mean it was Niels," said Jeff.

"I have no other explanation. And now, in his guilt, he believes her spirit haunts this station."

"I'm sorry."

"It doesn't help us to dwell on it. I just wanted you to know. That same day, we lost long range communications."

"A glitch?"

Hideo shook his head. "The relay panel is missing."

He tapped a key on the keyboard and an audio spectrogram popped up on screen. He pressed the spacebar and a low-frequency rumble played from the speakers. The line in the middle of the spectrogram wobbled slightly with bass-filled undertones. Then it spiked as a metallic screech swelled and vanished.

"This is the signal Sandra recorded before she went missing," said Hideo. "We managed to send it back home before we lost comms. Their response was...curious. Does this sound mean anything to you?"

Jeff listened a moment longer, then shook his head. "Should it?" he asked.

Hideo muted the signal. "I had hoped so. After all, it's why they sent you all this way."

"What are you talking about?"

Hideo sighed. "I'm not surprised they didn't tell you. Who would travel all this way if they knew the truth?"

"Hideo, come on."

"The powers-that-be think the signal is meant for you," he said. "They want you to go outside and talk to the alien."

13

KATE

"Samples!" shouted Santi as he bounded through the camp. "I have more samples!"

Kate stood outside her long canvas research tent, watching his approach with a smile on her face. He deftly side-stepped government workers and science professionals who were rushing about their own business within the small city of similar tents that had been erected almost overnight after Kate arrived two weeks ago.

Since then, she had spent eighteen hours a day with her attention split between the ground and the sky.

Kate shielded her eyes from the beating Sun and wiped dirt from her chin. Her team had been experimenting with the saplings again, planting a fresh line of them for testing inside the greenhouse section of her research tent. Brighton's government contacts were handling the dirty work within the crater, while most of Kate's team had been tasked with monitoring the approaching comet and figuring out the effect the blue plasma from the impact crater was having on Earth's flora.

Her initial assessment was that it killed everything it touched.

Santi Nangolo held out a cardboard box for her, his face beaming with pride.

"All the way from the University," he said.

"I thought the Colonel didn't want any third parties involved."

"He is desperate, according to his own words. I know many people there. They are good people."

"Is that where you went to school?" Kate asked, accepting the box.

The Namibia University of Science and Technology was nine-hundred kilometers north, in Santi's hometown.

"That's where I was going to school when all this happened," he corrected, gesturing toward the meteor crater behind him. Still many friends there."

Neesha emerged from the tent behind Kate, wiping her hands. Her black hair was up in a messy bun and dirt smudged her cheeks.

"Oh, hey Santi," she said. "Want to help me with the trees?"

His smile almost split his face in half.

"Of course I do!"

They ducked back into the tent, leaving Kate holding the box of samples. She lifted the lid to find three rows of vials, each one containing the glowing blue substance that arrived with the meteor.

The heart of the meteor recovered from the crater was mostly unremarkable. Over ninety percent of it was iron, and the other ten percent was comprised of easily identifiable materials that offered no explanation as to the meteor's origin. Brighton's government scientists were still trying to figure out why it didn't cause more damage on impact, but so far they couldn't offer a single working theory.

Kate carried the box of samples into the tent and set it atop the stack of empty boxes she'd been collecting since she arrived.

Wasting no time, she withdrew the first sealed vial and studied its label. It described the date and depth at which it had been taken. This one was the deepest she'd seen—scraped off the crater wall nearly one hundred meters below the surface.

One of the biggest surprises to her, and to everyone else who visited the meteor impact site, was the depth of the hole. Instead of creating a wide, relatively shallow bowl upon impact, the meteor had somehow drilled one-hundred-and-twenty meters into the ground at a forty-degree angle.

Brighton's engineers had rigged an ingenious tube system out of thick, clear plastic so workers could descend into the sloping tunnel without being exposed to the blue substance. There were sample collection sites along the tube that allowed one to reach out through a self-sealing diaphragm to scrape goop from the tunnel walls.

The entire mouth of the crater was covered by a rigid inflatable dome, with a clean room on one side where hazmat suits were donned and disposed of. They were never reused.

On the far side of the long tent, Neesha and Santi

struggled to drop the root ball of a heavy sapling into the hole she'd spent the last hour digging. The ground near the impact site was hard no matter where one stabbed it with a shovel.

Between them and Kate were a series of metal tables scattered with the equipment of discovery: microscopes, sample centrifuges, even a rock tumbler.

Kate carried the vial over to a transparent box on the nearby table. Inside the box was a series of tubes and compartments on one side, and a small terrarium on the other. A layer of soil covered the bottom of the terrarium, out of which a leafy plant grew, reaching up for the lights lining the roof of the box.

Kate inserted the vial into a slot on the side, and a protective shield slid over it. With a mechanical whir, the vial twisted in place as a needle penetrated its seal and dipped down into the glowing blue substance.

Soon, a steady trickle of the blue goop was suctioned through the tubes and compartments inside the box, moving from one to the next as the areas behind it were sealed off. All told there were thirteen layers of quarantine before the substance reached the terrarium.

Neesha and Santi appeared on the other side of the table, leaning down close to the box. The light from within lit their sweaty faces and reflected in their curious eyes.

The first drop of blue fell from a hole in the roof of the terrarium. It struck a leaf of the plant and splatted onto the soil.

More drops fell. Soon it was raining blue inside the box.

Within seconds, the leaves began to curl and blacken. The blue substance sank into the soil, seemingly crystallizing and turning it into an oddly-reflective, transparent gray.

Kate sighed and stood up, cracking her back.

"That was the last of the stomata blockers. We now officially have nothing that will slow this blue stuff down once it makes contact with a plant or tree."

"Or grass," Santi added.

"We should bury the crater," said Neesha. "Dump a million tons of dirt on top and quarantine the whole site."

"It's not this one so much as what's still headed our way," Kate replied.

"The Colonel said it was an Extinction Level Event," said Neesha. "Big enough to vaporize everything on the planet."

Kate nodded. "If the Odyssey can't stop it, yeah. But let's say they manage to knock it off course, and maybe a chunk breaks loose. If that chunk is big enough and hits us, we're going to need all the information we can get our hands on. How are the saplings coming along?"

Neesha sighed. "Two more to go."

Kate strolled to the entrance of the tent and took her floppy hat from a hook on the wall. "I'll leave that in your capable hands."

"Hey, where are you going?"

"To talk to the Colonel. We need more sealed

injectors for the trees."

I also want to look at the crater, she thought as she emerged into the sunlight.

Kate had found herself drawn back to the meteor impact site over and over again since her arrival. At Brighton's request, she was one of the few civilians who could enter the quarantine dome. He spent a lot of his time in a hazmat suit on the edge of the crater, overseeing the various operations involved on the scene.

As she walked through the camp, it was impossible not to think of it as an archaeological dig site. It was a dusty environment. Most of the tents were canvas, and many of the people scurrying around the site wore what she would consider traditional archaeologist attire—traditional meaning what she had seen them wear on TV.

Someone called to her from the entrance of a nearby tent. Her radio analyst, Rajesh Nanjani waved to get her attention.

"How's it going, Raj?" she asked as he held the door flap open.

Kate stepped into the dark tent, happy to trade the cool, stuffy air inside for the stifling heat outdoors.

"Big news," he said, hurrying past her. "*Big* news."

He shared the tent with several analysts from other teams. One of them nodded at Kate in acknowledgment, but the others didn't look up from their work. Raj sat on a tall stool at one of the long tables stacked with equipment. To Kate, it looked like an overly-complicated home stereo system.

Raj placed a large set of headphones over his ears and began twisting dials on the equipment. Several tablets had been daisy-chained to function as a multiple-monitor setup. He swiped each screen to pull up a kaleidoscope of data readouts.

"I detected the signal when I first arrived last week," he said, precisely turning a dial.

"Using my scanner," someone said from the next table over.

"Not now, Steven," Raj scolded.

Kate glanced between the two men as Raj continued.

"At first, it seemed benign. A simple FM band signal being emitted by the blue substance in the crater. It was not dissimilar from the signals scientists detected emanating from Io or several other moons in our solar system. Just a byproduct of their composition, yes?"

"You've mentioned it before," said Kate.

"Right," he said, holding up a finger. "But wait. If I widen the scope to monitor a broader wavelength, I get *this*."

He took off his headphones and handed them to Kate. She lowered them over her ears and heard a soft, static-laced crackle over a deep, constant background thrum.

"You hear how wide it is?" Raj exclaimed, smiling. "It sounds like it would fill a concert hall."

He unplugged the cable and stuck it into another machine, then gently turned up the volume.

"And this is what you get when you narrow the spectrum so tightly that you shouldn't be able to hear a thing."

He tapped a button on one of his tablets and an ear-splitting shriek blasted over the headphones.

Kate yelped in surprise and slapped them off her ears. Raj laughed and almost fell off his stool.

"I'm sorry!" he said, waving his hands. "I'm sorry, it was too loud. But you see?"

"What was that?" she asked, handing him back the headphones.

His laughter quickly faded and he sobered up instantly.

"The real signal. I've spent all my time analyzing the broadband, assuming it was all data that was going out, if it was anything at all. But this is like a laser. Very narrow, very focused. And if you follow it as it goes into space, you'd expect to see at least some widening of the beam. But no."

"What does that mean?"

"It means it's artificial. Not from a natural source."

"There's nothing else in the crater besides the blue stuff."

Raj shrugged. "Then that's what's causing it. Kate, I don't think it's a data stream. It's the same kind of narrow beam the military uses when they laser-paint a target for a missile launch."

"It's a beacon," she said softly. "The signal is guiding the other comet."

14

JEFF

"I can't believe I'm doing this," said Jeff.

Hideo checked the seals on Jeff's spacesuit as they floated in front of the inner airlock door.

"We are almost in a stationary position beside the alien creature," said Hideo. "Venus Lab can only maintain this lower altitude for fifty minutes before it must return to higher orbit. We can't spare the fuel."

Jeff laughed and shook his head. "I still don't know what I'm supposed to do out there."

"Neither do I," said Hideo. He cast a quick glance at Erikson, who still snored softly in his sleeping compartment. "Hopefully it will become clear to you when you are outside of the station."

"You mean before or after the thing eats me?"

"I don't think you believe that will happen." Hideo tapped a few commands on Jeff's wristpad, then nodded with satisfaction. "I'm going to suit up as well, just in case you need me. If not, I'll be ready to let you back in at a moment's notice."

Jeff pulled on his helmet and slid the neck lock into place. "Can you hear me?" he asked.

"I hear you," Hideo replied, his voice tinny and

distant inside Jeff's helmet.

"What's your official job on this station?" Jeff asked.

"Data analyst."

"And Erikson? Sandra?"

"Systems Engineer and Project Specialist."

"Any of you have kids?"

Hideo frowned. "Is that relevant?"

Jeff smiled sadly. "I hope not."

A countdown timer on his wristpad beeped, and he turned to face the airlock door as Hideo swung it open. Jeff slowly drifted into the spherical airlock as Hideo sealed him inside.

"You will be approximately five kilometers from the creature when you emerge from the station," Hideo told him.

Jeff nodded to himself as the white halogen lamp in the wall flicked to yellow while the airlock depressurized.

"Expect a seven-minute journey, depending on how close you want to get," Hideo continued. "I recommend not getting too close. When you're at a comfortable distance, we can try sending it the same frequency that got a response last time."

"Fool-proof," Jeff said, more to himself. "What could go wrong?"

"Ready? Here we go."

The outer airlock door swung open silently.

There was a good reason Venus was the third-brightest object in Earth's night sky, Jeff realized as he drifted from the airlock. Thick clouds completely covered its surface, brilliantly reflecting sunlight.

Those clouds amplified the greenhouse effect on the surface, causing temperatures to rise upwards of eight-hundred degrees Fahrenheit. It was the hottest planet in the solar system because of it, though Mercury was nearer to the Sun.

Jeff had grown accustomed to looking down on Earth over the last few months while he worked on the new space station. As he stared at Venus, it was easy for him to envision Earth being swallowed by poisonous clouds of sulfuric acid in a similar manner, the surface eventually cooking beneath a thick blanket of atmosphere until all life was choked from existence.

Had that happened here? he wondered. *Is Earth another Venus waiting to happen?*

Jeff thumbed his control stick and his pack let out a spurt of nitrogen, pushing him away from the station. He drifted along the length of the thermal antimatter drive attached to the stern of the *Seeker*. Two-meter tall block letters on the hull proudly proclaimed *DEEP BLACK*.

Jeff passed the engine wash housing at the end of the antimatter drive, and then he saw the alien.

His breath briefly caught in his throat as suppressed memories flooded into his brain simultaneously.

—running across the breaking, shifting frozen surface of Titan as the alien passed through one torus after another, growing and changing with each emergence—

—saying goodbye to Tag and Noah inside the

<small>Samuel Best</small>

torus before trying to find his way back to Earth—

—standing with Kate on the floating debris of an oceanic research station as the alien emerged from a giant torus in the water and disappeared into the sky—

He shook his head to break the trance and thumbed his control stick.

"Proceeding," he said.

Red light glowed within deep cracks of the alien's exterior, dimly illuminating the pitted, igneous-like outer shell or skin. Its shape defied easy explanation. Its body was tube-like—roughly the length of a football stadium—perhaps eighty meters in diameter at its widest point, with a slight pinch in the middle. Each end tapered down to points that were sharper than they were blunted, but not precisely sharp. A pool of lava-like substance covered the end of the alien aimed toward Venus.

The outer shell or skin seemed to have an almost faceted appearance anywhere it wasn't scored by deep chasms, as if it were comprised of a million smaller flat surfaces. If pressed to put it into words, Jeff would say it looked like a stretched-out hour glass without as much squeeze in the middle, and with a half-rocky, half-faceted surface instead of a smooth one.

He maintained a steady speed of approach. His wristpad relayed information to the visor readout in his helmet, which told him he would reach his desired distance in four minutes.

"Jeff," said Hideo over the comm channel. "Why did you ask about our children?"

104

"I shouldn't have said that, Hideo. It was careless."

There was a pause, then: "I would like to know."

Jeff made a slight adjustment to his course and took a deep breath, letting it out slowly.

"Are you aware of the details surrounding the first mission to Titan?"

"Only what was declassified two years ago."

"That's about a quarter of it," Jeff told him. "We encountered a torus not long after parking in orbit. And also another ship. Before we arrived, the torus had swept over the other ship, killing everyone inside. It also killed our commander."

"Riley," said Hideo.

"Yes. And at the end of that mission, one of them got me, too."

There was a long silence before Jeff continued.

"Two survivors from my crew made it safely to a ship and went home. But three of us on that mission returned to Earth with the help of a torus. Out of everyone who was killed by the torus, only Riley, myself, and a crew member from the other ship were sent back. We were the only ones without children."

Jeff slowed his rate of approach. The alien steadily grew before him, and now he could discern a slight pulsing sensation from the lava trails in its surface.

"The tori are machines," Jeff continued as he tapped on his wristpad. His pack spat nitrogen and he slowed to a stop. "They were designed to bring this alien back to life. As a side-effect of their programming, I believe they treated us like organisms that hadn't fulfilled our ultimate purpose."

"Procreation," said Hideo. "Everyone who had produced children never came back."

"In its machine reasoning, those people had ticked that evolutionary box," Jeff replied. "The three of us who returned were brought back because we had unfinished business, is maybe the simplest way I can say it." His eyes ran the length of the alien's body as the clouds of Venus moved slowly in the background. "But it's just a theory," he mumbled.

"I have two boys and one girl," Hideo told him.

Jeff smiled. "I wouldn't worry about it, Hideo. I don't think they kill us on purpose, at least not anymore. When we encountered the torus on Titan, it was collecting materials to build human drones for use on the surface. We can manipulate objects much easier, move around quicker...and we're easy to replace. When it killed the crew of the other ship, and Commander Riley, it was gathering the pieces of a puzzle. Now that it has all of those pieces, we don't have anything to worry about."

Another pause.

"Thank you, Jeffrey. Are you ready to proceed?"

"I'll open up all my comm channels. Not sure what I can do beyond that."

"Okay. Sending the frequency in three...two...one."

A soft crackle of static played over the comm channel.

"I don't hear anything," said Jeff.

"The frequency is outside our audible range."

"Is it sending back the signal?"

"Not yet."

Jeff let out a spurt of nitrogen from his pack and drifted closer. He was five kilometers away, and the alien appeared as large as a fifty-story skyscraper if he had been standing right under it.

"I don't remember it being this big," he said. "I think it's grown."

The red glow from the deep cracks in the surface of the alien dimmed until they went black.

"Did you see that?!" Jeff asked.

A metallic screech filled his helmet, and he screamed in pain, instinctively putting his gloved hands to the sides of his face shield. The screech faded and was replaced with a gentle, low-frequency *thrummmmmmm.*

"That's the signal," said Hideo. "It's talking back."

Jeff shook off the piercing echo of the metallic screech and tried to pop his ears.

"Now what?" he asked.

"Try talking to it."

Jeff cleared his throat, feeling more than a little ridiculous.

"Hi," he said stupidly. Then he addressed Hideo. "Can you record over that?"

"Already done."

"I appreciate it. Okay, starting over." He cleared his throat again. "This is Jeffrey Dolan. I would like to extend sincere greetings from Earth. That's the blue-green one next door."

Erikson's sleepy yet still disapproving voice came on the line. "Oh, well done, Mr. Dolan."

"It doesn't know what we named the planets," Jeff said in defense.

"Move closer," said Erikson.

"No."

"Then this exercise is pointless."

"Give it time, Niels," said Hideo.

"Oh, so *now* you're talking to me?"

The red glow returned to the cracks in the alien's skin. Instead of the slow, steady, heartbeat pulse from before, the light cascaded along its length, starting at the pool of red lava-like material at its "nose" and sweeping back to its "tail". The sweep increased in speed, and seemed to Jeff to resemble a machine powering up to release a massive charge.

"I think it's time to—"

His next words were cut off when the power in his suit died.

"Hideo? Niels?"

The comms were dead. He thumbed the control stick but got no response.

A torus streaked into view from deep space and slammed to a stop next to the alien. The motion was so precise, so outside the realm of what should be physically possible, that it caused Jeff's mind to freeze while he struggled to make sense of the image.

A black membrane spread to cover the opening of the torus.

Blue light glowed from the middle of the torus, spilling across the alien's pitted exterior and tinting the clouds of Venus. A meteor identical to the one that hit Earth streaked out of the torus and punctured the planet's thick atmosphere, trailing blue plasma in its wake. Even after the atmosphere closed in to cover the tunnel it bore through the clouds, the brilliant blue comet was still visible as it plunged toward the surface.

The torus vanished as quickly as it had arrived, seeming to blink out of existence.

Jeff floated helplessly next to the alien. He tapped on his wristpad, but the screen was blank.

This is a real problem, he thought.

How long could he survive without the pack pumping fresh oxygen into his suit? Five minutes? Maybe six?

He had shaved off a minute of his travel time on the front end by stopping short of his destination, but that still left a little over six minutes of travel time to get back to the space station...assuming the power returned to his suit.

Without functioning heat elements in his gloves, a slight cold sensation began to creep over his fingertips.

Jeff tucked his knees up to his chest as best he could in an effort to spin around. It didn't have the exact desired effect, but he turned slowly just the same.

As he spun in slow motion, his gaze swept over the space station in the distance.

The lights were still on. They were probably calling to him to see if he was alright.

His spin turned him toward the alien. The red glow pulsed slowly from its open veins, and it remained unmoving.

When Jeff saw the space station again, a suited figure was drifting his way, holding a spare power pack. The figure was still minutes away.

Jeff blinked slowly as a wave of fatigue washed over him. His breathing became increasingly difficult, like trying to suck air through a wet cloth.

He was in a gentle spin. His vision dimmed to black while he looked down on the sunlight bouncing off the clouds of Venus.

By the time Hideo arrived, swapped the shorted-out pack for a fresh one, and switched on the circulation system, Jeff was unconscious.

15

RILEY

The cabin lighting in the *Odyssey* had switched from emergency red back to surgery-room white, indicating that, at least for the time being, no more micrometeors were on an impact course with the ship.

"Only the starboard-side impact ruptured the hull," said Riley. "I can't find the other two, and sensors are kicking back a single breach."

Commander Brighton didn't seem to hear him. Her gloved fingers flew over the control console as she calculated an unplanned reverse burn more than a day ahead of schedule.

"Why don't we just drop the bomb and get out of the way?" Piper asked.

"We can't place it when the ship's moving in the opposite direction," Brighton replied. "We have to reverse course first and match trajectory. The only way to be sure the comet will hit the bomb is if we drop it as close as possible. Then we clear out."

There was a grunt over the intercom.

"Miller?" asked Riley.

"Could use a hand," he replied, his voice strained.

Riley quickly unbuckled and drifted past Piper, still in her chair. She looked up at him, worried, and he offered her a small smile.

Miller was at the back corner of the crew cabin, straining to move a metal storage cube up the wall. Riley was about to ask him what he was doing when an empty juice sachet zipped past his helmet and vanished behind the container.

"It's a pinhole," said Miller, then he laughed. "But I still can't slide this stupid thing."

Riley floated over and grabbed the storage cube. Bracing his boots on the floor, he shoved upward. The metal cube scraped against the wall in protest as it slid millimeter by millimeter to cover the hole. As soon as it was sealed, the metal cube groaned from the stress and rapidly vibrated.

"How long until we can stop?" Miller asked.

"Six hours," Riley told him.

"Well, good thing this isn't the only storage cube."

Miller drifted away from the wall, revealing his hand that had been behind the crate, hidden from Riley's view.

It was covered in glowing blue goop.

"Hey now," Riley said in surprise, slowly drifting back. "Whatcha got on yourself there, Sergeant?"

Miller looked down at his hand. "Oh, yeah. This was all over the wall near the hole." He wiped his glove across the chest of his spacesuit, smearing a bright streak of blue.

"Don't do that!" Riley ordered. "Don't put it

anywhere else."

A look of concern crept over Miller's face as he looked at his gloved hand. "Why, what is it?"

"We don't know. Are there any backup spacesuits on this rig?"

"Three."

"Can we risk getting out of our suits with that hole in the wall?"

Miller looked at the metal storage cube covering the hull breach. "Smarter to wait..." he hesitantly admitted.

"The suits are designed to keep stuff out," Brighton's voice came over the intercom. "We'll keep you strapped into your chair until we fix the breach, Miller. Then we'll swap out your suit."

"Copy," he said.

He almost patted Riley's shoulder as he drifted past, then remembered the goop and shrugged.

After he was gone, Riley used his wristpad to switch to the secure comm channel that only he and Brighton could access.

"Commander?" he said.

"I'm here."

"Any word from home about what that goop might be?"

"Not a clue. But we don't have a quarantine room and it's all hands on deck."

"Understood. Out."

He switched back to the ship-wide comm channel.

"Piper, report to the work lab."

"On my way."

"What's going on?" asked Brighton.

"All hands on deck, remember?" Riley replied.

"Just tell me if you're planning anything stupid."

"Who, me?"

Riley drifted aft, into the galley and work lab. Piper arrived a few moments later.

Her linguistics equipment was arranged in a neat cube behind the work table, secured to the wall with thick black straps.

"What have you been working on recently?" asked Riley.

"I'm coding an algorithm to scan for patterns in the data Colonel Brighton sent me. Patterns lead to character discovery, and that leads to an alphabet."

"It's that simple?"

She laughed, surprising him.

"Sure," she said. "'Simple'."

"Do you have anything ready to go?"

She drifted closer and grabbed the edge of the table. "Why?"

"After that micrometeor shower, I don't know if we'll get another chance to test your equipment. If anything you have in your bag of tricks has a chance of working, I don't think we should wait on it."

"I agree," Commander Brighton chimed in.

"Can the equipment interface with the ship systems?" asked Riley.

"I modified it for that purpose before leaving

Earth," Piper answered, not without a hint of pride. She pointed at a workstation built into the wall next to her stack of equipment. "I can use that console right there."

"Plug it in and send it out," Riley said. "Let's at least give it a shot before we're smashed to smithereens."

Piper clapped her gloved hands together. "Good. I was starting to feel like a vestigial organ."

"Gotta flip around for the burn soon," Brighton warned.

"Five minute warning?" said Riley.

"You got it."

Piper worked quickly, unhooking the black straps one at a time and securing her equipment to the work table. It all looked like different-sized boxes to Riley. Cables snaked out of each one, and Piper plugged them all into a long black panel that she kept strapped on top of the equipment pile. A thick red cable ran from that panel into the ship's workstation.

Piper called up an interface on the workstation screen that Riley had never seen before.

"What's that?" he asked.

"You like it?"

"I don't know what it is."

"It's my program. It runs the equipment from a graphical interface instead of me having to manually adjust each one."

Riley floated over the table, looking down at the varied boxes.

"What do they do?"

"If I told you that, I'd have to kill you," she said brightly.

"Right."

She pointed at the boxes in turn. "This one's the brain, this one's the brawn, and this one is my secret ingredient. I'll give you a hint. It weighs a ton, powers the other two, and rhymes with 'mattery'."

"Please don't kill me over that," said Riley.

"Commander," Piper said. "You might see a slight draw on your computational reserves."

"Already seeing it. How much will it drop?"

Piper swiped through screens on her workstation and tapped an icon.

"That's all."

"Ship can handle it. Proceed."

"How long will the message take to get there?" Riley asked.

"At this distance, not long."

"What's it say?"

"It's all mathematics. If there's anything sentient inside that comet, it shouldn't be hard to miss."

Riley chewed on that thought for a long moment. "And what if there's nothing sentient inside?"

She smiled again, only this time it wasn't because she was happy.

"Then I didn't need to come along after all."

Riley spread out his arms, gesturing at the ship.

"Yeah, but...adventure. Excitement. Right? How is that pointless?"

Her eyes met his, and she gave him a genuine

smile. "It's not," she admitted.

"Whenever you're ready," said Brighton. "We have to burn."

Piper typed on her keyboard workstation, swiped away error messages from the screen, then pushed a large green thumbs-up icon.

"Away she goes."

Riley waited.

"So that's it?" he asked. "Now what?"

"Now we wait for an answer," Piper replied.

"Everyone back to the command cabin," said Brighton. "Strap in for the burn."

Riley gestured for Piper to go first, and she mock-curtsied as best she could in her bulky spacesuit.

Halfway through the crew cabin, Commander Brighton gasped in surprise over the intercom.

"Riley!" she yelled.

He pushed Piper's boots from behind, launching her forward. Riley pulled on a handhold in the wall and flew into the command cabin. He hit his chair with an *"Oomph!"*

"Look," said Brighton, pointing to the cockpit window.

A brilliant blue fireball swelled around where the comet had been moments before. At that distance it was no larger than a ping-pong ball. The explosion quickly collapsed on itself and vanished, leaving behind three distinct, glowing blue embers.

"Is that it?" Piper asked as she strapped into her seat. "Did it blow up?"

Riley forced his eyes from the window and called

up the long-range visual scans on the control panel.

He swallowed hard as he studied the incoming data.

"No. It didn't blow up. It split into three pieces. The system is telling me at least one of them is still headed for Earth."

"Relay the info back home," said Brighton, swiping at her console. "They can give us a new trajectory if we need it. In the meantime, let's get this ship turned around."

Piper drifted next to Riley and grabbed his shoulder for support as she looked at the three comets.

"*Mon Dieu...*" she whispered.

Riley glanced sideways at her. "Maybe it was something you said."

Commander Brighton tried to suppress a laugh and failed. Piper looked at her, mouth open in shock, then at Riley.

"This is no joke!" she protested.

Riley couldn't help himself. He started laughing, too.

Soon Piper was smiling, shaking her head and chuckling softly. She tried to wipe away a tear pooling at the corner of her eye but her hand bumped her face shield, which made her laugh even harder.

"Miller, you want to get in on this?" said Riley.

The sergeant had been silent the entire time.

"Miller?"

Riley floated over to the sergeant's chair and looked in through the face shield. Miller was unconscious, his head cocked back at an odd angle in his helmet. Globs of dark blue liquid floated out of his open mouth.

"Commander," Riley said slowly. "We have another serious problem."

16

KATE

The rigid inflatable dome over the impact crater was opaque white, preventing satellites and news crews from constantly trying to catch a glimpse.

Kate flashed her badge at the entrance to the clean room outside the dome and began the hasty process of donning a blue hazmat suit. The room was divided into two sections, with a clear wall between them. While Kate slipped into her hazmat suit and struggled with the seal, someone on the other side of the wall peeled theirs off. They dropped it down a chute which led to an underground collection bunker. Where it went from there, Kate didn't know. Perhaps the used suits were put into sealed toxic waste barrels and buried elsewhere.

The guard on duty buzzed her into the dome after she passed through the decontamination chamber.

"Come on, come on," Kate whispered, bouncing on the balls of her feet.

The situation inside the dome was remarkably calmer than the one on the outside. No one was rushing about like a chicken with its head cut off. In fact, she only saw three other people on the rim of the crater. One of them operated a pulley connected to a cable which disappeared into the crater. The other two were watching the other man pull the cable, chatting amongst themselves.

Kate stepped carefully to the edge of the crater. She had to push down the bottom of her voluminous soft helmet to watch her own feet.

A large plastic tunnel with transparent walls, wide enough for two people to walk abreast (if they could walk inside at all), descended into the crater. A string of lights attached to the roof of the tunnel illuminated the dark passage, along which ran a sectional ladder and a long ascension rope. At the bottom of the crater, one-hundred-and-fifty meters down, a brilliant blue light pulsed slowly, like a heartbeat.

"Back again?" said the Colonel from behind.

Kate was startled and her foot slipped over the edge. Brighton caught her arm and pulled her back.

"I'm sorry about that," he said quickly, adjusting the helmet of his hazmat suit. "I thought you would have heard me coming."

"I guess I was daydreaming," said Kate. She took a deep breath to calm her racing heart. Then she shook her head to clear it and remembered why she was there.

"Did you know about the signal?"

"You told me about it last week."

"I mean, did Raj tell you what he found? The narrow beam? It's a beacon for the larger comet."

Brighton peered over the edge of the hole.

"That's one working theory, yes."

"So you did know?"

"Kate, we're working on it."

"What does that mean?" she asked. "You know how to stop the signal?"

"Something is in the works. I'm sorry I can't tell you more about it."

"Why not?!" she almost shouted.

"Our work here must remain compartmentalized. Each team has a specific goal. There are a dozen reasons why, but I can't tell you any of them. I carved out a lot of leeway for the people here on the ground, but my hands are still tied in many ways. Speaking of teams, how's yours doing? Can I get you anything?"

Kate sighed, reluctant to let it go.

"We need more injectors," she told him.

He nodded. "I'll have a fresh batch sent over. Any progress?"

"We've exhausted our attempts to fortify native flora against the blue substance. If this stuff ever gets out, there's no stopping it."

The Colonel turned to face the crater, frowning.

"It's the same story from every camp," he said grimly. "I really hoped we'd find a way to neutralize it."

"Neesha says we should bury it. Maybe that would mute the signal."

The Colonel knelt down at the edge of the crater and scooped up a handful of grayish, crystalline powder. It slowly fell through his gloved fingers, glimmering in the light from the overhead halogen lamps.

"This was all green," he said, standing back up. "Lush farmland. It's not the impact we have to worry about, Kate. It's what this blue substance does to our soil once it's here. That's the real threat."

"It changes our soil," said Kate. "It sucks out the oxygen and alters its structure."

"Which in turn affects our air," Brighton added.

"But why?" Kate asked. "I don't see the point."

"I'm no scientist, but I would think the first part of moving to a new planet is changing the thermostat to a more comfortable temperature."

"The alien," Kate said quietly. "I thought it was near Venus."

Brighton shrugged inside his blue hazmat suit. "Some people have a summer home." After a pause, he said, "I'll get you those injectors."

He walked away, leaving Kate alone, staring down into the darkness of the pit. The blue heart at the very bottom gently pulsed, and she found herself unable to look away.

On the other side of the hole, one of the three men near the pulley shouted for help.

The sleeve of his hazmat suit was caught in a clamp on the pulley line. From the look of it, he had been trying to free an empty sample bucket from the clamp and reached too far.

The pulley line moved continuously on its track. The man's tiptoes dragged across the ground as he slid toward the edge, screaming. Behind him, the other two men leaped forward, each grabbing a leg.

They were also pulled toward the ledge. Soon, the man with his arm stuck in the clamp hung over the open pit. The other two men let go of his legs when they realized they would go over the side as well. They scrambled back as the man over the pit swung forward after they released him. His legs went up toward the roof of the dome, then came back down hard.

His suit ripped away from the clamp and he fell.

"He'll hit the safety net," Brighton said through clenched teeth, suddenly at Kate's side once more. He pushed a comm button on the neck of his hazmat suit. "This is Colonel Brighton. We need medics and quarantine personnel to the dome, right now."

A ring of nylon mesh encircled the pit five meters down, sticking out from the edge at a ninety degree angle and stretching inward for two meters.

The falling man hit the sloping edge of the hole just above the safety net and bounced right over it.

"Oh no," Kate whispered.

The man howled as he tumbled into the darkness. He smacked against the plastic tunnel descending into the pit and scrabbled to hold on. His hazmat suit squeaked against the plastic as he slid lower.

Then he slipped off the tunnel and fell into a puddle of blue substance.

The goop had pooled in a small nook on the side of the tunnel. The man stood up, staring at the arms and hands of his suit, completely covered by the glowing blue substance.

"Stay right there!" Brighton shouted down into the pit. "Someone's coming to get you out!"

The man looked up at the Colonel, but Kate could tell he wasn't really listening. He was terrified. After a moment of uncertainty, the man jumped at the plastic tunnel.

This time he caught a ridge where two sections had been sealed together. He clenched a fistful of the soft plastic on each side and pulled them apart, yelling as he strained.

"He can't rip that open, can he?" Kate asked.

"It's just plastic," Brighton replied in a grim tone.

A small hole opened in the seal. The man shoved his arms inside and widened the hole until he could slip inside. Holding the ascension rope which ran the length of the tunnel, he climbed quickly, his hands leaving smears of bright blue on everything he touched.

A group of soldiers burst into the dome from the clean room. Brighton held up his fist, telling them to stop.

"He's coming up the tunnel," he told them. "Who's on tranqs?"

"I am, sir," said one of the soldiers, stepping forward and showing his tranquilizer gun.

"Okay, Marsh. Good. Nobody else shoots unless I say so," the Colonel ordered. "He is not to reach that clean room."

The two men who had been working on the pulley stumbled toward Kate, dumbfounded.

"What's his name?" she asked them.

"Ed," one of them replied.

Kate peered into the pit. Ed was almost to the top of the plastic tunnel, a look of sheer panic in his eyes.

"Ed!" she yelled. "Listen to me!"

He stopped climbing and looked around until he found her.

"We'll get you out of that suit, but you have to be calm!"

He shook his head and continued his climb. Grabbing the platform at the top of the hole, he hoisted himself up and quickly got to his feet.

"Stay right there, Ed!" Kate shouted.

The soldiers behind her advanced. Ed saw it, too, and ran around the opposite side of the crater, toward the clean room.

"Marsh!" barked the Colonel.

The tranquilizer gun puffed smoke twice. Two tranquilizer darts struck Ed in the chest. He stumbled forward, still trying to run, and fell facedown on the ground, an arm's-length from the clean room door.

"Get a containment unit in here, now!" Brighton ordered.

"What will happen to him?" Kate asked.

The Colonel sighed with exhaustion. "I hope we don't have to find out."

17

JEFF

Jeff awoke shivering in a sleeping bag. Someone had stuffed him into it and zipped it up to his chin. He balled his hands into fists and slowly opened them. They felt like blocks of ice.

Niels Erikson floated in a seated position next to him in the corridor, his legs crossed and his hands gently resting on his knees. His eyes were closed and he appeared, for once, almost serene.

"Hideo brought you back," he said without opening his eyes. He pulled off his wireframe glasses and wiped the lenses on the breast pocket of his green nursing scrubs. "You were almost dead."

"My suit power cut out."

Erikson nodded and opened his eyes. Despite the wild tufts of white hair sticking out behind each temple giving the doctor a manic appearance, Jeff could tell that something had changed.

"The lights flickered in the station when the comet passed. If we had been closer, I have no doubt we would have lost power as well."

Jeff shifted in the sleeping bag and groaned in

pain. Pins and needles jabbed his entire body as the numbness began to wear off.

"You have a strong constitution," Erikson commented. "Someone more fragile, like myself, probably would not have made it back alive...even with Hideo's intervention."

"Where is he?" Jeff asked.

"Back in his isolation room."

Jeff gave up trying to get comfortable and relaxed, allowing his body to float loosely inside the sleeping bag. He closed his eyes and tried not to think about the pain.

"He still thinks you killed Sandra."

"He doesn't want to think it," Erikson replied, "but he thinks he has to."

"What about the comet?" Jeff asked.

Erikson uncrossed his legs and grabbed a handhold along the corridor wall, then pulled himself slowly toward a laptop workstation near Jeff's sleeping cubby.

He adjusted his glasses and typed on the keyboard. "We don't know much. The station doesn't have the equipment for external sampling. We have video feeds, but I can't analyze substance. There's no way to see the comet's core. Sandy would know more about it, but..."

"It was the same as the one that hit Earth," said Jeff.

"And it might not be the last."

"What are you talking about?"

"As I said, we do have video feeds outside the

station."

He unclipped the laptop from its workstation and spun it so Jeff could see the screen. It showed a black expanse of pinpoint white stars, and a single blue dot in the middle.

"I take it that's not Earth," Jeff said.

"No," Erikson replied. "It most certainly isn't."

"Bigger than the last one?"

"Orders of magnitude bigger. Until several hours ago."

He tapped a button and the blue dot split into three distinct points of light.

Jeff rubbed the stubble on his chin. "It broke apart? That's a good thing, right?"

"This is where it gets tricky," said Erikson.

He called up an image of the solar system on the screen. Wide arcs tracked the orbit of planets around the Sun. Erikson tapped a key and three blue dots labeled "X" popped up on the screen. Their trajectories were calculated to sideswipe the Sun by a mere hundred thousand miles before impacting Mercury, Earth, and Venus.

"Is that simulation accurate?" Jeff asked.

Erikson nodded. "Three planets. Three comets."

"Then I have to send a message back to Earth!" said Jeff urgently.

Erikson floated away from the workstation. "Oh, what's the rush? Their comet is smaller now, anyway. But go ahead, if it makes you feel better. I would guess they already know."

He hummed softly to himself while he opened a

sachet of orange juice and ducked into a sleeping cubby.

Hideo floated past the window of the supply room at the end of the corridor. He appeared to be talking to himself.

As Jeff pulled himself quickly down the corridor, toward the airlock, he wondered if isolation inside a small space station would turn anyone quirky like it had these two. In the past, astronauts had done longer tours closer to Earth, but they had more people inside the station and faster communication with home. Venus Lab was humanity's first real experiment in distant space habitation. Jeff understood that it was bad enough being so far from Earth, but to lose long range communications as well certainly didn't help the situation.

He drifted into the airlock and closed the door behind him, then waited as the system cycled through its required integrity checks. A green light flicked on next to the door in the *Seeker*'s hull, and Jeff went inside the ship.

The air inside the *Seeker* was cool and stale. He sealed the door behind him and strapped himself into the command chair, then powered up the systems. The control panel flickered like a faulty fluorescent light.

Jeff frowned. He had never seen that before. Usually the control panel lit up instantly. He swiped away some routine notification boxes and called up the communications interface.

There was one audio message waiting for him.

Jeff tapped it, and a quiet static filled the cabin.

"It's me," said Kate. "Your ship has been sending back routine check-in pings, so I know it's in one piece. I just wasn't sure about you. This is not an official message, by the way. This is an I-miss-you message. Brighton would probably frown at my personal use of resources, but one of the perks of running a private space company is being able to talk to whoever you want. You're so far away that it almost makes me wish there was a torus near you so we could communicate with each other instantly."

Jeff smiled.

"Just kidding," said Kate. Then she sighed. "Too much has been going on here for such a small message like this one. I'll send you a data packet with the latest updates. Did you find out why Venus Lab hasn't been communicating? We're all antsy for an update about what's happening out there."

While she spoke, Jeff began the process of collating the ship's data for transmission back home, including the new information Erikson had just shared with him.

"Yes, we know about the other comet," Kate went on.

Three comets, now, Jeff silently corrected.

"It's moving so unnaturally fast, Jeff," Kate continued. "We don't have time to send another ship to Venus Lab. The Seeker only holds two, and there are four of you."

Three of us, thought Jeff. *Sandra is gone.*

Kate paused for several long moments, then she sniffed. Jeff could imagine her wiping her nose and trying not to cry, but when she spoke again, her voice was firm and confident.

"I know you'll do everything you can for everyone on that station. I just want you to do the same for yourself. Please be careful. I love you."

The message cut off.

Jeff sat motionless for a long time, his finger poised over the transmit button on the control panel.

As soon as he sent the message, Kate would know there was a comet streaking toward Venus, as well as Earth and Mercury. He didn't want to add that on top of the stress she was already juggling, but he had to warn someone.

He transmitted the data packet to Earth, then called up the ship's systems interface on the control panel. If there was a way to squeeze three people into the *Seeker* for a trip back home before the comet hit Venus, he would find it.

18

JEFF

"The problem is the oxygen scrubbers," said Jeff.

He floated with Dr. Erikson in the central corridor of Venus Lab after returning from the *Seeker*. The door to Hideo's supply room was open, but he was nowhere to be seen.

"All three of us could fit in the ship," Jeff said. "It would be cramped, but it's nothing the two of you aren't already used to."

"What about the scrubbers?" Erikson asked.

"They're not compatible with the ones on the station. In other words, I can't remove the ones from the lab and use them on the Seeker."

"Not even with some modification?"

"Square peg, round hole," Jeff replied. "In this case, the peg is too square to retrofit."

Erikson frowned. "What about the spacesuits? Could we wear those?"

"Only enough extra packs for thirteen hours, if you're lucky," Hideo shouted from his room. He drifted past his open door, intently focused on prying at a metal box in his hand with a screwdriver.

"That's nowhere near enough time to cover the two-week journey," Erikson groaned.

"There's something else we need to think about," said Jeff. "What if there's no Earth when we get back?"

Hideo stopped fiddling with his metal box and looked up slowly. He emerged from his room to float next to the others.

"I hadn't thought of that," Erikson whispered.

"The other ship," said Hideo.

"What other ship?"

"The Odyssey."

"Riley's crew," said Jeff.

"If the comet is headed toward us," Hideo said, "then the Odyssey must set a course to pass Venus."

Jeff chewed his fingernail in thought.

"Depends on fuel, timeline, our own orbit. They might need to slingshot around Venus to get to the comet. They wouldn't be able to slow down."

"What about on the way back?" Erikson asked.

"If they come back," said Hideo.

Erikson *tsk*ed. "Don't be a pessimist."

"I'm a realist, Niels."

"If they come back, it's a possibility," Jeff admitted, "but a distant one. I'm going back to the Seeker to see if I can come up with another idea."

A metallic *clunk* echoed in the corridor. The three men looked at each other in confusion. Erikson shrugged.

Clunk.

"Where's that coming from?" Jeff asked.

"Outside?"

"No," said Hideo. "Down there."

He pointed to the other supply room at the end of the corridor. The door to the dark room was sealed.

Jeff drifted down the corridor and bumped gently against the door. He pressed a button near the handle and the lights inside flickered on.

The room was empty.

Clunk.

The noise sounded like it came from inside the thick metal door.

Jeff turned around slowly to face the other two.

"I'm going to try something," he said carefully, watching their reactions. "It's not going to make any sense at first. I promise I'll explain everything when I get back."

"Back from...where?" Erikson asked.

"I'll explain that, too. Just be calm when I go."

While Erikson sputtered demands for an explanation, Jeff closed his eyes and entered fold space.

When he was brought back from Titan after the first mission, he returned with a small black sphere, about the size of a golfball, embedded at the base of his skull. Riley had one, too, along with anyone else brought back by a torus. Presumably, the spheres were implanted in every human drone the tori manufactured. They allowed the drones to utilize fold space—a multidimensional tactic of creating multiple instances of a room or area in the same three dimensional space.

The drones were everything the impassive machines could not be: dexterous, agile, and dispensable. The tori created soulless human automatons to build vast, complicated structures on the surface of Titan—structures that facilitated the rebirth of an extinct race.

After years of practice, Jeff could create several instances of a room on top of itself, and even use the separate instances to store different items. He thought of it as unlimited closet space.

Whenever he closed his eyes and entered fold space, the sphere in his skull became cold. It emitted a low-grade electrical current, about the same as one would feel licking a 9-volt battery.

There were no visuals associated with multiple fold space rooms. It wasn't as easy as calling up a screen where he could see different video feeds as if he were observing multiple security cameras.

But he could feel it.

The instances spread out like a deck of cards, and each card had a texture in his mind. At home, in Florida, the hallway closet had five instances stacked atop one another. Whenever Jeff needed access to one of them, he had to "feel" the texture. He came to know which one held the vacuum, which one was full of his long-sleeved shirts, and which one Kate used for storing their Christmas decorations.

Jeff had no way of knowing if there were any other fold space instances on Venus Lab. He certainly hadn't created any. Yet, with the alien creature so close—a being that had undoubtedly mastered fold space to the point of imparting it to the tori, and by extension, the human drones—the entire solar system could very well be stacked on top of itself multiple times.

The one instance inside Venus Lab Jeff could sense had a texture that was almost empty...but not completely.

He shifted over to that second instance. Erikson and Hideo vanished in the blink of an eye.

The station was empty of everything that wasn't structural, gutted of all its loose electronics and equipment.

Of course, thought Jeff. *They're all in the other instance—the one with Niels and Hideo.*

He spun slowly in place, inspecting the corridor. It showed the same smudges near the missing workstations where someone had repeatedly attached and removed a piece of equipment.

That meant the instance was created recently, and Jeff could guess exactly when.

Clunk.

He peered through the window of the empty supply room at the end of the corridor.

A woman floated inside. A wall panel had been removed and tumbled in slow motion behind her. She touched two exposed electrical wires together and another clunk sounded from inside the metal door.

The woman was in her mid-forties, with frizzy brown hair that was half-tamed by a loose hair tie. She wore a dirty orange coverall and suffered from obvious malnourishment. Her face was ashen, her lips parched. She stared off into nothingness as she touched the wires together to a slow, slow rhythm.

Jeff opened the door and waited.

The woman paused as she was about to touch the wires together. She dragged her gaze away from the distance and her eyes eventually met Jeff's.

"Sandra?" he asked.

"Please tell me you brought water," she whispered hoarsely.

"No, but we can get some right now."

He held out his hand, but she passed out before she could take it. Jeff drifted over to her and gripped her shoulders. He closed his eyes, and switched back to the other instance of Venus Lab.

19

RILEY

Sergeant Kenneth Miller lay on the work table in the lab, held down by several of the thick black straps Piper used to secure her equipment to the wall. The inside of his face shield was a dark blue smear.

Riley had volunteered to be the one to move the sergeant from the command cabin to the back of the ship. In zero gravity, it was easy enough to gently guide the sergeant by only occasionally tapping the bottom of his boots.

Carol Brighton, Piper, and Riley floated around him at a distance, staring at the blue smear on his face shield.

"I thought you said the suits were designed to keep things out," said Piper.

"They are. But clearly it doesn't apply to whatever is on that comet," Brighton replied.

Riley glanced at Miller's wristpad.

"The sergeant's heart rate is slowing," he said. "Oxygen levels in the suit are dropping, and he's barely breathing."

"What do we do?" Piper asked nervously.

"I've been trying and failing to think of a way to get him out of the suit without touching the blue stuff," said Brighton. "We can't risk anyone else touching it, so we keep working." She checked her wristpad. "The ship will be at full stop in less than an hour. First priority is patching the hull. Then we run a systems check, primary burn, and drop that bomb."

"I'll patch the hull," said Riley.

On the table, Miller jerked once against his restraints and Piper screamed.

"Sergeant, can you hear me?" said Brighton.

Miller's body went limp.

"But he's the bomb guy," Riley said.

Brighton sighed. "Then we don't have much time to learn everything we can about our payload. I'll pull the schematics."

"What about me?" Piper asked.

"Stay with Miller," Brighton told her. "I'd like someone by his side in case he wakes up."

"Is it...is it safe?"

"Just don't touch him," said Riley.

Piper swallowed hard as she looked at the sergeant on the table, then nodded.

An hour later, Riley was in space, coasting along the hull of the *Odyssey* while trying his best to ignore the trio of blue sparks in the distance that seemed to grow larger with every passing second. Despite his intent, he couldn't help but wonder which of the three was barreling toward his ship.

He gripped the bulging tool bag containing his patch kit in one hand and operated his suit controls with the other.

Commander Brighton's voice came in over his headset.

"Temporary patch on the hole inside," she said. "I'll shore it up after you're done out there."

"Copy," Riley replied. "Approaching the breach."

The stubby starboard fin gracefully bulged from the hull a little more than halfway from the nose. A black pockmark marred the otherwise smooth surface. A swath of vibrant blue, plasma-like material had been slapped across the hole as if flung by a paintbrush.

He grabbed a recessed handhold a meter away from the gentle rise of the fin and bumped to a stop against the hull. After hooking his safety tether to the handle, he fished around inside his full tool bag, pushing aside various pneumatic and hand-powered tools, until he found the bolt gun. He connected the tube on the bottom of the gun to a small container of compressed air strapped to his utility belt.

Riley let the bolt gun drift free, tethered by its tube, and he closed his eyes.

The base of his skull went ice cold. Goosebumps surged over his body. He jerked once in his suit, as if zapped by an electric shock.

He opened his eyes slowly, then reached back into the tool bag. A rigid piece of FlexPanel the size of a shoebox lid was the only thing inside.

Riley smirked.

He hadn't needed to use his fold space ability in a long time. In fact, he actively avoided it. There were a lot of unnatural circumstances involved in his resurrection after he died on the first mission to Titan, yet the fold space ability seemed to push the limits of his acceptance.

His wife—before she became his ex-wife—used to say he was a simple man. Sometimes she meant it as an insult, but other times it was a compliment. Riley couldn't disagree. In retrospect, it was one of the few areas of common ground between them.

He closed his eyes again, switching to another instance of fold space he had created inside the tool bag. Reaching back in, his gloved hand bumped against the spare oxygen packs he had brought outside.

Ever since the adventure with Noah in the torus, he never intended to go EVA again without a healthy backup supply of breathable air.

The bolts were in the last instance of the bag he had stacked on top of the others. He carefully placed them on a magnetized strip on his spacesuit just above his utility belt.

Riley let out some slack in his safety tether, drifting closer to the hull breach. The blue gunk painting the hull reflected brightly in his face shield. He tapped a command into his wristpad, and his pack spurted nitrogen to stabilize him in front of the hole in the hull. Riley touched the middle of the FlexPanel to the hole. It slowly curled in at the edges until it was flush with the edge of the stubby fin.

After pulling off a cord around the edge of the panel to release the strong adhesive, Riley methodically loaded eight bolts into the bolt gun, one after the other, and fired them through the FlexPanel and into the hull. His pack streamed nitrogen with each pull of the trigger, keeping him from spinning away from the *Odyssey*.

"Breach sealed," he said.

"Copy," came the quick reply from Brighton. "I'll finish the one in here."

Riley drifted away from the blue patch of glowing material on the hull, eyeing it with suspicion.

He swapped his bolt gun for a drill when he arrived at the access panel under the starboard fin. The bit spun slowly, drawing out the long bolts that secured the panel. Riley flipped it open and poked his helmet into the shallow maintenance cubby.

"Starboard O-2 scrubber intact," he announced after calling up its status on a touchscreen inside the maintenance hatch. "Everything in the green."

"Miller's gone," said Piper, her voice thick with emotion.

Riley's gloved finger paused over the touchscreen.

"There's nothing solid inside his suit," Piper continued. "It's like he disintegrated in there."

After a long silence, Riley said, "I'm all done out here. Returning to airlock."

He sealed the maintenance panel and secured his tools.

As he neared the airlock, the HUD readout inside his helmet flashed bright red.

"Riley, get in here now!" Brighton screamed over the comm channel.

"What is it?" he asked, jamming his control stick forward with his thumb.

"The comet is accelerating. We have to move or it will smack right into us."

Riley was going too fast. He hit the airlock door and tumbled past it. With a loud curse, he overcompensated, sending himself spinning away from the ship.

"Now, Riley!"

"Open the hatch!" he shouted.

He manipulated his thumb control stick until he faced the ship, slowing his backward trajectory. He mashed it forward and shot toward the airlock door.

It cracked open slowly. Riley's eyebrows went up as he quickly approached, unsure if it would be open in time.

His left shoulder slammed into the edge of the hatch as he coasted inside the airlock, spinning him sideways. He crashed against the inner airlock door with a shout of pain, his helmet cracking against the curved wall.

"Close it!" he yelled.

The hatch lowered slowly, sealing out the black void beyond.

"Riley, I'm sorry," said Brighton. "I have to burn."

"Give me time!" he said, turning to face the airlock controls.

"Don't have it. Brace yourself."

He stopped fumbling with the controls and looked around the airlock in a blind panic.

Three backup spacesuits hung like scarecrows

144

within recessed cubbies carved out of the aft-side airlock wall. They vibrated as the *Odyssey*'s engine warmed up.

Riley kicked off the wall and landed on one of the suits, his impact cushioned by its many layers of shielding.

He quickly ripped the other two suits off the wall and laid them over the first, creating three layers of padding. Riley put his back to the padding and, gripping the handholds on either side of the recessed cubby, sank himself into the suits until his helmet knocked against the wall.

The engine fired.

Riley was only able to scream for a moment before the air was crushed from his chest. He squeezed his eyes shut against the pressure that made it seem like they would flatten against the back of his sockets.

The chairs in the command cabin absorbed most of the vibrations during a primary burn. Riley was in direct contact with the wall of the ship, and his bones rattled. He clenched his jaw shut tight but his teeth knocked together with the speed of an ultrasonic dental cleaner.

Commander Brighton's voice was a distant echo inside his helmet.

"Burn complete in three...two...one."

The engine cut out, plunging Riley's world into screaming silence. He went limp inside his suit as he drifted out of the recessed cubby.

After sucking in a deep, painful breath, blackness

crept in from the edges of his vision. His head lolled in his helmet and he lost consciousness, floating inside the airlock.

20

JEFF

Hideo kept his distance from Sandra as she took small sips of lemonade from a sachet. He watched her warily from the corner of his eye, his arms crossed over his chest, as if he wasn't convinced it was really her.

Erikson, by contrast, could barely contain himself with enthusiasm.

"I don't believe it!" he kept saying. "I absolutely don't believe it!" He gripped a handhold on the corridor wall and would pull himself closer to Sandra, studying her face, her hair, her hands. "Oh, Sandy, I just don't believe it!"

"Neither do I," she whispered.

Hideo drifted a little bit closer to Jeff.

"You disappeared," he said.

"Yes, I did."

"And then you came back in the supply room with Sandra."

"It's called fold space," said Jeff. "It's a...a gift from the torus that brought me back to Earth. They put something in my head. A small black sphere that allows me to perform the same trick."

Jeff paused.

"Well, don't stop there!" Erikson said with excitement.

"I saw the phenomenon inside a torus during my first Titan mission," Jeff continued. "The tori were using fold space to store hundreds of biological samples in a room that could only hold twenty. Somehow the tori are able to stack the same version of a room on top of itself. If you know how to travel between the stacked rooms, you get infinite storage space."

"There was no torus here when Sandra vanished," Hideo said.

"But the alien was," Jeff replied. "Sandra, what were you doing when it happened?"

Her hands shook uncontrollably as she took another sip of lemonade.

"I was...I was testing signal frequencies. Trying to find a way to communicate with it. When I set our dish to receive, I discovered it was using our own long range communications to send out a signal."

"A signal to where?" Hideo asked.

"Earth."

"Hmm," said Erikson. "So you removed the long range comm relay."

"And tossed it out the airlock," Hideo added. "That's what I heard when you disappeared."

"That was dramatic of me, but yes," Sandra admitted.

"It could have been trying to communicate," Jeff

said.

She shook her head slowly, with obvious effort. "It was the same signal the comm satellites picked up in Earth orbit right before the comet hit."

Erikson looked from her, to Jeff, to Hideo. "But what does that mean?"

"It's a pilot signal," said Hideo. "A guide for the comet to follow."

"The bigger comet," Erikson said quietly. "One of the three."

"I sent the same signal back to the creature," said Sandra. "Except I forgot to adjust the delay. Instead of the wavelengths cancelling each other out, they were amplified."

"You poked the hornet's nest and got stung," Jeff said.

Sandra nodded. "It obviously didn't like what I did."

"Wait a second!" Erikson said, holding up a finger. "Fold space. We can use it to duplicate the oxygen scrubbers in your ship!"

Jeff shook his head. "It doesn't work like that. It won't create matter by duplicating objects. If I put a box in a room and create another instance of that room, the box won't be in both places."

Erikson's shoulders fell. "And now there are four of us."

A heavy silence hung in the air.

"Can we move Venus Lab out of the comet's trajectory?" Jeff asked.

"To what end?" Erikson replied. "Without a

planet to orbit, we're adrift in space. Eventually our oxygen will run out."

"It would buy us some time until the Odyssey could pick us up on its way back. I sent a request in the last data packet to Earth."

"I'll start crunching numbers," said Sandra.

She winced as she grabbed a handhold in the corridor.

"Not alone, you won't," Erikson told her.

He gently took her hand and guided her to a nearby workstation.

Jeff drifted over to look at the screen but Hideo got in his way.

"You have to go out and try again," he said. "We have limited options, and we need to exhaust all of them."

Jeff searched his face to find any hint that he was joking.

"Last time I went out there I got sideswiped by a comet and almost died."

"Statistically, it won't happen twice," said Hideo.

"Until that big one gets here."

"There is still time. Besides, I have an idea on how to get the creature's attention."

Jeff sighed. "Oh?"

"Is the fold space technology limited to enclosed spaces?"

"I'm not sure. I've only ever tried it inside a room, and that's tricky enough."

"Never outside, in an untethered space?"

"Never had a reason to, I guess."

Hideo smiled. "Now you do."

Which is how Jeff Dolan found himself outside Venus Lab in his spacesuit, approaching the alien for a second time.

"But this time I'll be fine," he mumbled to himself. "Because this time I have a box."

It was a metal container the size of a shoebox. Hideo had cut a hole in one side and stuffed a receiver, a speaker, and an LED flashlight inside. The speaker played a distorted version of the signal that had caused the alien to create another fold space instance within Venus Lab. The flashlight beam shone through the hole in the box, and was just for presentation.

Jeff adjusted his angle of approach and swung wide in front of the alien, placing himself between it and Venus.

Looking at the creature from a hundred meters away, at what Jeff assumed was head-on, all he could see was an oval pool of dark lava-like material, edged by an ellipse of rock-textured skin.

Jeff held the box out and released it, giving it a gentle spin. The flashlight beam glided over his bright orange spacesuit while the speaker relayed the signal Sandra was sending to the receiver from Venus Lab.

With a small spurt of nitrogen from his pack, Jeff moved away from the box. He spun around when he was ten meters away, then he stabilized.

"Here goes nothing," he whispered.

He closed his eyes and slipped into fold space.

The sphere in his skull turned to ice.

And suddenly he was falling into an abyss, plummeting down even though he couldn't fall in space, screaming and clawing at the air as he was yanked deeper and deeper into a never-ending pit—

Jeff sucked in air and opened his eyes. He was breathing heavily, and sweat pouring down his face inside his helmet.

The box was still there, spinning slowly. The alien hadn't moved.

"Jeff, are you okay?" Hideo asked from the station. "Your heart rate just went through the roof."

"Yeah," Jeff said between breaths. "Just...experimenting."

He had tried to grapple with too large of a space, he realized. Whenever he used fold space to create another instance of a room, he had six walls to contain the duplicate. In the vastness of space, there were no limits.

He decided to focus on the spinning metal box.

Jeff closed his eyes and pictured it tumbling in slow motion. The sphere at the base of his skull shocked him as he created another instance of the box's interior.

That was the easy part, Jeff thought.

Instead of filling an instance to fit inside the walls of a container, Jeff tried to expand the instance he'd created beyond the walls of the cube. If he could get it past the metal walls, the box should—

It disappeared.

"Woo!" Jeff shouted in surprise.

The red light glowing from the cracks of the alien's skin dimmed to black. It contracted at the middle, both its ends retreating slightly inward. They pushed back out, elongating the creature and narrowing its midsection.

Venus disappeared, plunging Jeff into darkness.

He thumbed his control stick and slowly turned around in disbelief. The stars were gone as well, and so was the space station.

The creature drifted closer. The red light in its skin intensified, shining out from the deep cracks until they bathed the alien in a bright red glow.

Jeff was alone with the creature in an infinite void.

Well, I wanted its attention, he thought. *Looks like I have it.*

21

JEFF

Jeff thumbed the control stick attached to his glove. Nitrogen spurted out from the waist of his spacesuit, but he didn't move farther away from the alien.

The red light on its igneous skin pulsed like a heartbeat. Its lava-filled maw now appeared the size of a football field. Jeff felt himself hopelessly drawn toward it—or was the creature moving toward him? Everything else in the universe had blinked out of existence. With no frame of reference, it was impossible to tell which one of them was moving.

Jeff had tried backing away from the creature, but he had yet to try going over it. He manipulated his control stick and a steady stream of nitrogen spat from the bottom of his pack. He drifted up, rising past the creature's maw, until he was looking down the length of the alien from above.

A vibration took hold in his feet and traveled up his body, shaking his bones and his vision. He stopped in place despite the nitrogen shooting out of his pack.

Jeff cut the stream and the vibration stopped.

"Okay, okay," he whispered. "I'll stay put." He raised his voice and said, "Can anyone hear me? Hideo? Sandra?"

The line was dead.

"What about you?" Jeff asked, addressing the alien. "Anything you want to say?"

The little metal shoebox suddenly reappeared in front of Jeff, still spinning and sending the flashlight beam into the black.

Jeff concentrated and accessed the instance of fold space he had created around the box. It was much easier than last time—like slipping into a pair of comfortable shoes.

The box vanished. Despite himself, he grinned.

The box reappeared.

Is it playing a game? Jeff wondered. *Or are we talking?*

He decided to try sending it mental images. Jeff closed his eyes and imagined the shoreline near Kate's old condo in Florida. Waves gently lapped the shore, and gulls called in the distance.

He opened his eyes.

Nothing.

"We need to know what you're up to," he said loudly. "That comet is going to wipe out our species if we can't stop it. You used our planet to come back to life. Seems only fitting that you don't let it be destroyed."

Venus blinked back into existence.

Jeff stared at it in wonder. The clouds were gone.

There was no visible atmosphere. He had a clear, unobstructed view of the brownish-red surface.

Nearly every bit of that surface was swarming with activity.

Jeff was too far away to make out the little details, but he could tell that a network of sprawling complexes was being built, all of them interlinked by straight runs of black material hundreds of kilometers long. Tiny specks moved in swarms over the emerging complexes, adding more material to the mass.

The landscape below was dominated by a torus the size of North America, seemingly embedded on its side into the surface of Venus. Despite being buried half inside the rocky surface, it spun slowly in place.

Arches of black material emerged from the void that stretched across its inner hole, curving up toward the empty sky before curling back to the ground.

The swarms formed clouds around these arches, harvesting the material at a pace equal to their emergence from the black hole at the center of the giant torus.

Next to the torus, a small patch of blue glowed like a beacon.

The comet impact site, he thought.

Jeff watched the civilization spread before his eyes.

A bright blue light bloomed from behind.

A comet a third of the size of the planet streaked down to the surface and impacted where the smaller

LAST CONTACT

one had fallen. A blue explosion blinded Jeff, and he turned his head away.

When he looked back, the clouds of Venus returned in a flash, then disappeared again with a blink, as if someone had flicked a light switch on and off. Each time they disappeared, the blue plasma carried by the comet had spread farther across the surface, like a creeping fungus.

It happened again: the clouds blinked into existence, then vanished.

"It's not a civilization," said Jeff. "You're terraforming."

Venus disappeared.

"What about the comets?" Jeff asked.

Several minutes passed with no response.

Jeff maneuvered along the length of the creature until he was over its middle. Then, before he could second-guess himself, he drifted closer.

Up close, the alien's skin was indistinguishable from the jagged surface of a rocky asteroid. Jeff intended to maintain a distance of a few meters away, but as he got closer, he felt the unmistakable pull of gravity.

He fired a strong burst of nitrogen to back away, but he was inexorably drawn to the surface. He bumped into it between two deep crevices, each glowing red from their depths. Clumsily, Jeff pushed himself to his feet.

Either gravity or some other force was indeed keeping him pinned to the alien. He tried a little test jump and floated upward, then gently came back

157

down.

Jeff turned in place, surveying the terrain. It all looked the same from where he stood: a hard, rocky shell split by deep cracks filled with lava.

With a grunt, he knelt down.

"Not sure if this will work either," he said, "but I'll try anything at this point."

He placed his gloved palms against the alien and closed his eyes. In his mind's eye, he quickly replayed all of his experiences with the tori, going all the way back to his first mission to Titan. Jeff imagined he was standing once again next to Kate on the debris of her ruined floating science lab as the alien emerged from a torus in the Gulf of Mexico. He recalled meeting himself on Titan—coming face to face with one of the countless drones that had been created to build alien machinery on Saturn's largest moon.

When he had run through his entire history of encounters with the alien culture, Jeff slowly opened his eyes and stood.

Venus was back in place, complete with its bright, reflective cloudy atmosphere. The stars had returned as well.

And there, too, was Venus Lab.

"—effrey, are you there?" said Hideo over the comm channel.

"I'm here."

"Our equipment went fuzzy for a second. Is everything okay?"

Jeff pressed his control stick and jumped up. He felt none of the gravitational pull toward the alien's surface. He easily drifted away, heading toward the space station.

"I think we need to get ready for that other comet."

22

KATE

His name was Edward Condon.

Colonel Brighton had him placed in a quarantine tent separate from the rest of the camp. The infected man was inside a metal lung with a long observation window.

As Kate watched, his hazmat suit had been peeled off by robotic arms inside the metal lung, revealing that the blue substance had penetrated his protective covering. Ed's arms were dark blue from his fingertips to his shoulders. Blue veins reached across his chest like the branches of a dead tree.

Three medical technicians huddled over a monitoring station behind Kate. Colonel Brighton leaned against the metal lung, staring in through the window.

"Two weeks," he muttered. "We went two whole weeks without something like this happening. Should've made the safety net wider."

Ed jerked within the metal lung and Brighton jumped back. Alarms blared from the monitoring equipment, then fell silent just as quickly.

"What was that?" Brighton asked the medical team.

"I don't know," said one, turning to her colleague. "Seizure?"

"Maybe," he said, struggling for an answer. "Maybe not."

"Look at his chest," said Kate, stepping closer to the window.

Ed's body went taut. He clenched his fists and twisted his head from side to side, the cords in his neck bulging.

His pectoral muscles turned blue before their eyes, as if dipped into a vat of ink. The blue spread down his stomach, and Ed started to convulse.

"Sedate him," said Brighton.

"He is sedated!"

"More!"

The blue on his chest turned dark purple and seemed to crystallize, forming a surface like that of amethyst. Ed arched his back, then went still. The skin over his chest crumbled inward, almost like sand falling through an hourglass, exposing his ribs.

Kate covered her mouth with her hands and stepped back slowly.

"He's gone," said one of the medical technicians.

"Asphyxiated," said another in surprise.

"He suffocated?" Kate asked.

"That didn't look like suffocation to me," Brighton added.

The med tech pointed at one of the monitors. "The air inside the chamber is eighty-six percent nitrogen."

The Colonel squinted at the readout, mumbling numbers to himself. Without another word, he spun on his heel and hurried out of the tent.

Kate chased after him, plunging into the bright midday sunlight.

"Colonel Brighton!" she shouted.

"We were right!" he called back, shaking his head. "I hate being right about this kind of thing!"

She caught up with him but had to jog to keep his pace.

"Right about what?" she asked between quick breaths.

"It changed the composition of the air in his chamber," Brighton explained. "The blue gunk. It did the same thing when it chewed up the grass near the crater."

"It creates a chemical reaction with whatever it touches," said Kate.

"And the byproduct is air we can't breathe." He looked up at the sky as he stalked through the camp. "Imagine a comet the size of a continent hitting us and spreading that blue gunk all over the planet."

"It would change our atmosphere completely."

"We need to block that signal now. No more excuses from the pentagon, no more—"

A soldier ran around the side of the tent and barreled into the Colonel, almost knocking him over. The person didn't look back to apologize as they scrambled toward the edge of camp.

"Watch it!" Brighton hollered.

Someone shouted off to Kate's right. A group of people shielded their eyes from the Sun and pointed up.

A cluster of bright blue fireballs shot through the sky, directly toward the camp.

"Colonel!" was all she had time to say before the first meteorite slammed into the ground.

A woman screamed as dirt and debris exploded into the air.

"This way!" Brighton yelled.

Kate followed him through the maze of tents, headed away from the primary impact crater. The meteorite that just hit had to be smaller than the first, or else there would be a lot fewer tents still standing.

More screams to her left as another meteorite hit. A pillar of broken wood flipped through the air and slammed into her side, sending her flying into a tent. The tent cords snapped and the canvas collapsed on her after she hit the ground.

She groaned and rolled out of the fabric, her left arm bleeding.

"Colonel!" she shouted.

No answer.

"Kate!" Neesha yelled from somewhere nearby.

Kate slowly got to her feet. "Here!"

A third meteorite hit, this one farther away, closer to the crater.

Neesha came running around a corner, her eyes wide with fear.

"There you are!" Neesha yelled, leaping into Kate's arm and hugging her fiercely.

"*Ow ow ow ow!*" Kate groaned.

Neesha released her. "I'm sorry! What's going on?!"

"Where's Santi?"

"We got separated. I don't know!"

"I have to find the Colonel," said Kate.

"He ran that way," Neesha told her, pointing in the opposite direction of the crater. "He was shouting your name."

"Okay. We need to get as far away as we can."

Kate grabbed Neesha's arm and pulled her toward the edge of camp.

She held her injured arm close to her body as she navigated the chaos. Smoke billowed from the fresh impact sites. More than once she had to step over a strand of blue goop snaking across the ground.

"Kate! Miss Jordan!"

Santi called for them from a distance.

They turned back as he ran through the camp, leaping over fallen support beams and dodging small puddles of blue goop. His skin and clothes were smudged with dirt, and he bled from a cut on his shoulder.

He smiled at Kate and Neesha as he came closer, now only fifty meters away.

"Santi watch out!" Kate screamed as a bright blue streak appeared above.

The basketball-sized meteorite sheathed in blue plasma hit the ground between them, shooting up boulder-sized chunks of earth.

Kate and Neesha were thrown backward from

the force of the impact. They tumbled across the dirt and came to a hard stop against the wheels of a military transport truck.

The impact site was shrouded in dust. It covered the area like a dark cloud. As the dust settled, the white inflatable dome covering the primary impact site became visible.

One of the meteorites had struck it in the middle, puncturing a gaping hole in the fabric. Parts of the dome billowed in the soft wind like a loose parachute, slowly deflating, peeling back to reveal the arching ribs beneath.

Kate and Neesha helped each other up, scanning the scene in stunned silence.

"Santi?" Kate said quietly. "Santi!" she yelled.

He coughed from somewhere in the ruin of the camp. The broken door of a refrigerator lifted from the ground, then fell back down.

Kate and Neesha ran over and lifted the door. Santi lay curled in a ball underneath, groaning. The side of his face bled from a deep cut, and he cradled his wrist against his chest. It was bent at an odd angle, the broken bone within pushing against his skin.

Neesha quickly bent down but Kate stopped her.

"Just wait," she said in response to the confused look from Neesha.

Kate performed a gentle examination of Santi, from head to toe, ensuring he hadn't been touched by a single drop of the blue substance.

"Okay," she said.

Together, she and Neesha helped Santi limp from

the camp. They joined a group of people far beyond the outer ring of canvas tents, collapsing to the dusty ground after the long walk.

Colonel Brighton sat nearby, glaring back at the site with a deep frown on his face. A med tech wrapped a bandage around his bleeding forearm. A matching wrap encircled his forehead, where a small patch of red showed through over his temple.

"The signal, Colonel," Kate said. She barely had the strength to speak the words. "We have to stop it now."

"Will you help me?" he asked.

Kate nodded, and so did Neesha.

Santi gave a thumbs-up from his prone position on the ground. Kate patted his shoulder, and he groaned.

"You need to get that wrist back in the right place."

At his request, the med tech helped Brighton to his feet. He dusted off the front of his uniform.

"We'll need one of those trucks," he said, pointing to the military vehicle Kate and Neesha had rolled into after the meteorite impact.

"I can drive big trucks," said Neesha.

"The last message I received from Washington said the comet headed for Earth was speeding up."

"No time to stand around jawing, then," said Kate.

"There's something else," Brighton said, looking right at her. "The Venus comet is moving faster than we thought. They don't have much time."

Kate stared at him, her mouth open in shock.

"I have to tell them!" she exclaimed.

Brighton nodded. "There will be a satellite radio in the truck. I can relay the message for you."

Kate ran toward the transport truck, Neesha and Colonel Brighton jogging to keep up.

23

RILEY

"Riley, time to wake up. Riley!"

His eyelids fluttered open. The world was a bright blur outside his helmet.

"Am I alive?" he croaked.

Commander Brighton's face sharpened in the blur. Piper was beside her. They were in the crew cabin, still wearing spacesuits, floating in the space between the sleeping cubbies.

"I tried to ramp up the burn as gradually as I could," said Brighton. "I'm sorry."

He tried to smile and failed.

"As long as we got out of there."

Piper and Commander Brighton shared a quick glance.

"What?" Riley asked. "What is it?"

"I ran a medical scan on you while you were unconscious," Brighton admitted. "You're hemorrhaging internally. The burn..." She paused and swallowed thickly, her voice on the edge of cracking. "The burn put too much pressure on your organs."

"I feel fine."

"Warmer than usual?" Brighton asked.

"Yes..."

"Inside your ribcage?"

"Oh, come on..."

"I'm sorry, Tag."

"Then why am I not dead already?!" he shouted.

"We don't know," Piper said gently, resting her gloved hand on his arm. "It might have something to do with what the torus did to you on Titan."

He clenched his jaw and shook his head.

"So the biological machine is broken," he said.

"There's something else," Piper hesitantly told him.

"Do go on."

"The comet is going faster than we are."

"It will overtake us in an hour," Brighton added.

Absurdity had a way of wiping out anger, and for Riley, in that instance, it worked like a charm. He barked laughter until searing pain exploded in his chest, forcing him to cough a small droplet of blood into his helmet.

"We should probably move out of the way," he said quietly, distracted by the blood droplet.

"We still have to release the fission bomb."

"Okay."

"It...it has to be prepped outside the ship," said Brighton.

"Of course it does," Riley snipped. "And why wouldn't it?"

"Miller's suit has the remote detonator."

He glanced back at the work lab. Miller's limp suit was still strapped to the metal table. Blue gunk coated his left arm, caking his wristpad.

"Well," said Riley. "No point in waiting around, is there? I'll do it."

"The engine is cold," said Brighton. "We only need to extend the bomb from the hold a few meters and release the clamps. After it's primed, you get back inside and we'll move out of the comet's path. It will overtake the bomb, and you know the rest."

Riley nodded and took a deep breath. Piper caught his eye and offered him a scared smile. He grinned back at her and winked.

"Everything's going to be fine," he told her.

And so Riley found himself back in the airlock, waiting for the hatch to open.

The warmth inside of his ribcage had taken on a very acute burning sensation, like a pool of acid slowly spreading out from the middle of his spine. The inside of his face shield was now covered with a thin constellation of blood droplets.

He hummed a soft tune while he waited.

"There are four clamps securing the bomb to the Odyssey," said Brighton over his helmet comms. "The control panel is on the side with two orange clamps."

"Copy."

"I'll relay the detonation code when you're at the panel. As soon as you hit confirm, come on back and we'll get out of here."

The airlock door slowly opened. Riley coasted into space.

"It doesn't feel like we're going ten thousand miles per hour," he said.

"You don't want to be out there for the next burn," Brighton replied. "You'd see what this baby can really do."

He turned his suit to face the back of the ship, and his breath caught in his throat.

The comet was larger than the Moon appeared from the surface of Earth. He had been outside not more than an hour ago and it was merely a spark in a sea of black.

A corona of blue energy shimmered around its edge, blurring space beyond. Explosions erupted from the surface like solar detonations, and were quickly swallowed back into the central mass.

"Now that is a sight to see," Riley muttered.

The fission bomb looked like a car-sized steampunk hourglass. It seemed as if a thousand different moving parts had been crammed into one dense package. On each side of the hourglass, metal tubes crawled over a solid black cube at the core.

The robotic arms holding the bomb were fully extended, reaching out from the open cargo hold as if making an offering to the void.

Riley coasted forward, slowing his momentum as he neared the bomb. He grabbed a handhold near the control panel and pushed a large green button on its left side. The screen glowed to life.

"I'm at the panel," he said.

"Releasing clamps now," Brighton said from inside the ship.

The four metal pincers silently released the bomb and retreated back into the cargo hold as the hatch closed.

"Ready for the code," said Riley.

Commander Brighton rattled off a string of number, letters, and symbols. After she finished, Riley pressed the button which read *Begin Countdown?*

The screen flashed red, and no countdown started.

"It didn't work."

"What do you mean?"

"Nothing is happening," he stressed.

"Um," said Brighton. "Hold on."

Riley pulled himself to the top of the bomb and looked back at the comet. It had swelled in apparent size since he last looked at it, bathing the *Odyssey* in bright blue.

"We don't have much time here, Commander," said Riley.

"I don't know, I don't know!" she shouted, flustered. "That's all it says in the schematics!"

Riley pulled himself back down to the control panel and rapidly cycled through the system menus. He found a log of error messages and read the most recent.

"It says 'awaiting input from second panel'," he said.

"What panel? I only see one."

Walking hand-over-hand, Riley pulled himself on top of the bomb and down to the other side.

Another control panel had been added to the bomb.

"Code again," he said.

Brighton recited it quickly.

Riley pressed *Begin Countdown?* on the second panel. It flashed red and spit out an error message.

"Come on!" he yelled at the screen.

He called up the error message and requested more verbose output. A line near the bottom of the message read simultaneous input required.

"You gotta be kidding me," he whispered.

"What is it?"

"The system needs two people to start the countdown."

"No," said Brighton in disbelief. "Miller didn't say anything about it being a two-person job."

"I will go," Piper said quietly over the comm channel.

Riley shook his head inside his helmet. "Piper, you stay right there."

"But you said you can't do it alone."

"I'll go," said Commander Brighton.

Piper raised her voice. "You have to fly the ship! If you die out there, I'm stuck here anyway!"

"It's mostly autopilot, Piper. You'll be fine."

"Please listen to her," Riley pleaded.

"NO!" yelled Piper. "I will not have come all this way for no purpose! Do you understand me? We don't have time to argue. I am going."

A minute later, Riley watched with dread as the

airlock door opened, and Piper emerged from the ship. Her eyes grew wide with terror when she saw how close the comet was to the ship.

"It's hot," she said. "Even through my suit."

"Pretty balmy out here, right?" Riley joked. "Go around to that side."

As Piper moved to the other control panel, the bomb drifted into Riley, bumping against his spacesuit.

"Hey," he said in surprise.

He looked down at the hull of the *Odyssey*. The ship slowly moved forward, slipping away from the bomb...and from Riley and Piper.

"Brighton, what are you doing?" asked Riley. "We're not done out here."

"I'm not doing anything," she replied. "Just waiting on you."

"The ship is moving away!"

"I'm still at the same speed."

"She's not moving away," said Piper, looking back. "The bomb is moving closer to the comet."

Riley realized she was right.

"Get back to the Odyssey," he said.

She met his eyes. "What's the code?"

Brighton began reading out the code. Static burst over the line as she recited it for the third time. With a few numbers to go, the line cut out.

"Commander?" said Riley, his gloved finger poised over the touchscreen.

Silence.

He moved to wipe sweat from his brow and his hand bumped against his face shield. Heat from the comet was cooking him inside his spacesuit. The space around him had been electrified by piercing blue light.

"She's too far," Piper groaned. "We can't make it back to the ship."

The bomb slipped faster and faster toward the accelerating comet. Riley could feel it drawing them in, pulling them closer.

The *Odyssey*'s orbital thrusters fired, trying to spin it out of the path of the comet. The thrusters burst nitrogen into space, but the ship remained where it was.

On instinct, Riley closed his eyes. A hammer of cold pounded his skull and surged down his limbs. They went numb despite the heat.

Piper gasped.

Riley opened his eyes, and the *Odyssey* was gone.

He felt blood trickle down from his nostrils.

"Type this in," he said to Piper, turning back to the control panel. He spoke the rest of the code from memory. "Ready?"

"Yes."

He pushed the confirmation button, and the screen flashed green. A five-minute countdown appeared on the screen.

"Up here," he said.

He pulled himself to the top of the bomb, where he met Piper. She grabbed his arms as he kicked off. The bomb quickly drifted away, falling toward the looming comet.

Riley jammed his control stick forward, letting out fat streams of nitrogen from his pack. They were useless against whatever force was pulling them into the comet.

"We're stuck out here?" asked Piper.

"Looks that way," Riley quietly admitted.

"What happened to the ship?"

"It's still there. You just can't see it."

Another droplet of blood fell from his nostril. The pain in his chest had spread throughout his body. His joints felt swollen to the point of bursting. He wasn't sure if that was because of the internal hemorrhaging, or the intense use of fold space to send the *Odyssey* into another instance of its own immediate location, or both of them combined.

"Carol is going to be just fine," said Riley. "After the comet passes, she'll fly right out of the little room I put her in."

"What about us?" Piper asked.

Riley closed his eyes. If he could tap into his fold space ability and send him and Piper to another instance of their four square meters of space, the comet, as far as they were concerned, would vanish.

After it passed, he could snap them back to the original instance.

He waited for the cold sensation to grow at the base of his skull, but he felt nothing.

Riley slowly opened his eyes to look at Piper.

"I can't," he said. "I'm sorry."

She pulled herself closer to him as they fell

toward the comet. Their face shields knocked together.

Tears pooled at the corners of her eyes. She blinked and they drifted in front of her face, where they quickly evaporated.

Piper turned to look at the comet, but Riley shook her arms.

"You look at me," he said firmly. "Piper, you look right at me."

He had never seen such fear as when she met his eyes.

"I'm afraid."

"I know," he said. She tried to look at the comet again. "Look at me. You're a hero, do you understand? Everyone on Earth is going to live because of what you did."

"You did the same thing," she said.

Riley smiled. "I died on my first trip to Titan. I was already living on borrowed time. Me dying out here...that's just tipping the scale back in the right direction. But what you did...you made a choice. A tough one. It was the right call. I don't know anyone else who would have done it."

Piper nodded, then began to cry. He held her as close as he could through his spacesuit.

"I'm so scared," she whispered.

"Me too. Just remember to look at me, okay? Don't look at the light."

She nodded again.

"I'll be honest with you," he continued. "It's probably going to hurt. But after that...after that it's not so bad."

She pressed her helmet into his chest.

He looked past her.

The comet filled his vision. He closed his eyes and it didn't make a difference—it burned just as brightly.

Squinting against the piercing light, Riley faced the comet. From his perspective, space had become an infinite canvas of burning blue. At the very heart of it, a sphere of plasma swelled into existence.

The fission bomb had detonated.

He held Piper close as they fell into the heart of the comet.

24

JEFF

"The comet is accelerating," said Erikson.

He floated near the door of the airlock while Jeff began the process of taking off his spacesuit. Hideo disconnected the pack and secured it to the wall while Jeff pulled off his gloves one finger at a time.

"We keep using the word 'comet'," Erikson continued, "which is obviously erroneous. Comets are ice and rock."

"Let's worry about nomenclature later," Jeff said. "When will it get here?"

"Sandy is still going over the copious amounts of data in the latest transmission, but it looks like one of the three comets will impact Venus in less than six hours."

Jeff and Hideo froze and looked at Erikson.

"Six hours," he repeated.

Hideo's laugh started as a low chuckle deep in his chest. He smiled and shook his head, then grabbed a handhold on the wall of the airlock and bellowed laughter, one hand over his stomach.

He sniffed abruptly and wiped away a tear. His

face became somber once more as he floated around to the back of Jeff's suit and began unfastening the insulating layers so Jeff could slip out.

"Mercury will be hit within the hour," Erikson added. He paused for a long moment while he studied Jeff. "Did you talk to the creature?"

Jeff slipped out of the spacesuit and pulled off his thick socks.

"Sandra needs to hear this, too."

The four of them gathered in the corridor of Venus Lab as Jeff relayed his experience with the creature. They listened intently, only interrupting to ask clarifying questions.

"It wasn't talking in the traditional sense," said Jeff.

"It definitely qualifies as communication," Sandra told him.

Erikson grunted. "Terraforming. It wants to live on Venus. On Venus!"

"Its species came from a volatile planet," Jeff said. "Volcanic. Primordial."

"Why send three comets?" Hideo asked. "Is it planning on terraforming Earth and Mercury as well?"

"It would seem that way," said Jeff. "The smaller comet that hit Earth is made of the same blue goop as the stuff I saw spreading over Venus when I was communicating with our big rocky friend out there. Kate said it changes the soil on a molecular level."

"Maybe more aliens are coming," Sandra offered.

"Or maybe it's not putting all its eggs in one

basket," Hideo replied.

Jeff frowned. "What do you mean?"

"Let's assume it terraforms all three inner planets. That doesn't mean they will all be perfectly suited for habitation. There will still be temperature differences based on their distance from the Sun. Each atmosphere would have to be individually tailored to provide the same living conditions on the surface."

Erikson scratched his cheek in frustration. "You're saying it's going to terraform three planets and pick the one it likes best?"

"Given how difficult it was to bring just one of the aliens back from extinction," said Jeff, "changing the atmospheres of three planets almost seems like it would be easier."

"There's something I don't understand," Sandra said. "Well, a lot of things, but this in particular. Where did the comets come from?"

"The alien homeworld?" Erikson offered.

"Jeff said it was only born five years ago," Hideo pointed out. "The comet is moving fast."

"I think," Jeff said, "this is part of a plan that's been in place for eons. The alien race constructed the tori when they knew they would go extinct. The tori searched for materials that would allow them to resurrect their own creators. The outpost we discovered on Titan was only one in a long chain of installations that served as a birth canal for the alien that emerged from Earth's ocean five years ago. Despite recent events, this species seems content to work on a cosmic timeline of thousands and thousands of years…and maybe longer."

"Well," Sandra said slowly, "we only have six hours. Let's talk about our options."

"We could break orbit and move to a safe, observable distance," said Erikson. "The Odyssey could pick us up on its way back to Earth."

"What if that ship is destroyed?" Hideo asked.

"Now is not the time for pessimism, Tanaka-san."

Hideo shrugged. "It's a valid question."

"Then two of us would be stranded until Earth sent another ship," said Jeff.

"And if there's no Earth?" Erikson countered.

"Let's focus on what we have control over," Sandra said. "We can move the station. We can leave the Seeker connected to the station for long range communication back home. If we survive the next six hours, then we can play 'what if'. Deal?"

They all looked at each other in silent agreement.

Sandra clapped her hands and rubbed them together. "Great," she said. "I'll start crunching the numbers to get us out of orbit."

"I'll pull the Seeker back to a safe distance while you maneuver," Jeff said.

"I will go over the data from Earth," said Hideo as he drifted toward his supply room. "Maybe we missed something."

Erikson floated in the opposite direction of Hideo. "And I'll run a systems check."

As Jeff turned to make his way toward the airlock, Sandra laid her hand gently on his forearm, stopping him.

"In case I forgot to tell you earlier," she said, "thank you for finding me."

Jeff smiled. "You're very welcome."

Sandra cast a furtive glance at Hideo, then at Erikson. She lowered her voice and drifted closer.

"Those two won't ever admit it," she said quietly, "but they've grown close during our time here. I feel like I'm the mother of two teenage boys sometimes, the way they fight. But I...I love them." She squeezed Jeff's forearm urgently. "And I want them to...if there was ever a choice between me or them, I would want them...to make it home." Sandra looked into Jeff's eyes. "Do you understand?"

He took her hands in his and gave them a comforting squeeze.

"We're all going home," he told her.

She smiled tightly and nodded quickly, then turned back to her workstation.

Jeff sealed the airlock behind him as he drifted into the *Seeker*. He secured his Constellation-class spacesuit and strapped himself into the command chair.

The control panel glowed to life under his touch, and he triggered the usual pre-flight diagnostics. Out of habit, he called up the communications interface, but there were no new messages waiting for him.

Through the narrow cockpit window, he saw a sliver of the space station, and Venus beyond.

All of our plans, he thought. *All of our scrambling, all of our struggles...and the planets just continue to spin.*

He was supposed to be in near-Earth orbit working on the shipyards. He never wanted to go so far away again...so far from Kate. Maybe if there was time after he moved the ship away from the space station, he would send her a quick message.

The control panel flashed green. Jeff initiated the undocking procedure.

"Venus Lab, this is Seeker. I'm going to put some distance between us."

"Copy that, Seeker," said Sandra. "We'll be joining you shortly."

As Jeff reached for the controls to decouple from the space station, a little yellow message box popped up on the display. He tapped it, a smile growing hesitantly on his lips in anticipation of hearing Kate's voice.

"Jeffrey, we were wrong," she said.

His smile vanished.

"We had estimates on the comet's speed based on apparent size. Our sensors can't see it so that's all we had to go on. But we've analyzed the data sent back from Riley's team on the Odyssey. Disregard our last message. By the time you get this, you'll have an hour, probably even less—"

The transmission cut out.

Jeff tapped the comms button and the control panel flickered. The lights in the cockpit dimmed, then came back.

A streak of vibrant blue shot past the cockpit window toward Venus. The cockpit lights flickered as another streak shot past.

Comet debris, Jeff thought. *Leading the big one.* He slammed his fist on the comms button. "Everybody to the Seeker, now!" he yelled.

25

KATE

The rigid inflatable dome was in tatters by the time Neesha drove Kate and Colonel Brighton to the other side of the impact crater. The half-moon ribs that arched over the pit were as white as bleached bone in the midday Sun. Shreds of coated nylon clung to the ribs, flapping like weathered flags in a light breeze.

"Here," Brighton said abruptly.

Neesha slammed on the breaks and Kate's hand flew up in front of her face to stop her forehead from banging on the dashboard.

"Sorry," Neesha offered, grinning sheepishly.

"Back it up to the big green tent. Don't stop until I say so," Brighton told her.

"Got it."

He popped the door open and jumped to the ground, motioning for Kate to follow.

The air was warmer than it was on the outskirts of the camp. A sharp chemical smell assaulted Kate's nostrils with each inhalation, burning her throat. She coughed until her eyes watered.

"Take this," said Brighton, offering a face mask.

It was the flimsy kind worn by surgeons during procedures, but she graciously accepted it and pulled it down over her mouth and nose.

The Colonel donned his and stepped back from the entrance of a large green canvas tent as Neesha swung the truck around and switched it into reverse.

He guided her back until the rear bumper pushed against the entrance. She stopped, but he kept waving her back. She shrugged, then rolled into the tent, popping seams and crushing support poles.

"Stop!" shouted Brighton, holding up his hands.

The truck was just shy of halfway into (or on top of) the tent. The Colonel hurried around to the back and lowered the gate.

"It's on wheels, so at least that's something," he said as he jogged past Kate.

She followed him to a part of the tent that hadn't collapsed: a large cube draped in loose green canvas.

Brighton flicked open a pocket knife and cut the fabric, walking around the cube shape until he could peel back the canvas to reveal what was beneath.

At first glance, it looked like a large water tank. The exterior was some kind of plastic shell, with a single wide touchscreen affixed to one side. If it weren't for the spray-painted skull-and-crossbones emblem over ominous stenciled letters which read EXPLOSIVES, Kate might have been fooled.

"It's a bomb," she said in disbelief. "Now why am I not surprised?"

"'When in doubt, bomb it out'," Brighton quoted.

"Push from that side."

They got behind the massive explosive and shoved until its wheels unstuck and it rolled toward the bed of the transport truck.

"You're just going to spread that blue stuff all over the place," Kate warned.

She winced as the bomb hit the truck's bumper with a loud *thoommm*.

"Which should scatter the signal," said Brighton. "We'll drop it right into the pool at the bottom of the pit."

Kate paused as Brighton climbed up into the truck bed and began to unspool a thick cable from a winch.

"Will that work?" she asked.

"One way to find out," he replied. "If we can trick it off course by even half a degree, we'll survive. Why? You got other plans?"

He handed her the hook at the end of the cable.

"Just under the plastic shell, at the bottom," he told her, pointing near the ground.

Kate knelt down and felt under the shell. Her hand bumped a metal hoop, and she connected the cable.

Brighton slid two ramps down from the back of the truck and grunted as he positioned the bomb's wheels at the base of them.

"What's going on back there?!" Neesha shouted from the cab.

"Loading now," Brighton called back.

He flipped a small switch next to the tailgate and

the winch slowly drew the cable back into the truck. The line went taut and, with a groan, the cube-shaped bomb rolled up the ramps.

Five minutes later, they were riding directly toward the pit, each of them casting the occasional worried glance at the bomb.

Kate pulled down her mask and tested the air: better than when she was standing outside, but not by much. Neesha had tied a pocket scarf around the lower half of her face, giving her the appearance of a bandit who had just stolen the truck.

"How far do we have to go after we drop it?" Kate asked.

Brighton checked his watch. "As far as we can. Everyone else should be at a safe distance already."

"Won't it blow up when it hits the bottom?" asked Neesha.

"Or melt in the blue stuff?" Kate added.

"No, and I don't know," the Colonel answered. "It won't blow until I activate the detonator."

Neesha didn't have to dodge too many obstacles on the way to the pit. Most of the tents had been blown down during the meteorite shower. The rest were deliberately struck or flattened by the drivers of other vehicles who took a more direct route away from ground zero.

"Here we go," Brighton said as they got closer.

Neesha slowed the truck and approached the pit at an angle.

"You two stay in the cab," said the Colonel. "I'm just going to shove that bad boy into the crater, then we high-tail it toward the others."

Neesha popped the truck into reverse and backed it up to the pit. She shifted into park as Brighton disappeared around the back. Kate watched in the rearview as he let the gate slam open, then operated the winch to let out some slack. After unhooking the cable, he tapped a sequence of numbers on the touchscreen attached to the side of the bomb. Fishing around under his collar, he pulled out a small electronic device attached to a lanyard. He held the device close to the touchscreen until there was a loud beep, then he gave the bomb a mighty shove toward the pit.

It rolled down the ramps, clattering against the metal, and hit the lip of the crater. The momentum flipped the bomb over the edge, and it vanished.

Brighton ran back to the cab and climbed inside.

"Hit it," he said as he slammed his door.

Neesha stomped on the gas pedal, the truck's tires spitting dirt into the pit after the bomb. The tires caught and the truck lurched forward.

Kate held on to the seat between her legs as if it were the saddle of a bucking bronco.

"How long until you can detonate?" Neesha asked.

Brighton checked his watch against a small glowing screen on the device he wore as a necklace.

"Less than a minute to clear the blast zone. It will be rough, but we should make it."

Neesha looked at Kate with wide eyes, and mouthed the word 'Should?!'

"You wanted to come along," said Kate, patting her leg.

Brighton checked the timer on his detonator.

"Almost there," he said. "And....now."

He entered a code on the small screen and squeezed the sides of the device.

Kate stared at one of the side-view mirrors, watching the bouncy reflection of the impact site.

Nothing happened.

Brighton frowned. He tapped the device screen again and mashed the buttons on its sides.

"Maybe we're too far away," said Neesha.

"Stop the truck," the Colonel ordered.

The truck was rolling to a stop when he jumped down to the dusty ground. Kate hopped down after him and stayed by the door as he stomped back in the direction of the site, removing the lanyard from his neck and holding the detonator high as if he were reminding the bomb who had his finger on the button.

A black streak shot down from the sky. It was a wide, blurred line that didn't so much travel from the sky to the ground as it did appear in both places at once, filling the space between with a semi-opaque black pillar.

The top of the streak dropped rapidly to meet the bottom, where it solidified into the object that had plummeted from the heavens.

A torus hovered directly above the meteor impact site, its obsidian ring slowly spinning. It was the same diameter as the thirty-meter hole in the ground. Kate had seen a much bigger alien artifact in the Gulf of Mexico. The torus from which the alien creature had emerged was one hundred meters in diameter. It would have dwarfed the torus looming over the ruined tent city.

Yet Kate felt the same dread she experienced five years ago. It crawled over her skin as a black film spread across the opening of the torus, filling the hole like ink spilled into water.

The torus rotated in place until it was parallel to the ground.

Kate looked down at her dirty shoes. Tiny pebbles danced atop the dirt. A fast vibration coursed through the ground, shaking her feet.

She ran forward and snatched the detonator from Colonel Brighton's outstretched hand.

"*NO!*" Kate screamed at the torus. "No no no no *NO!*"

She mashed the buttons on the sides of the detonator, then checked the screen. A green rectangle flashed the word *SUCCESS* over and over again, yet there was no explosion.

Kate howled in rage and threw the detonator at the torus in the distance. She collapsed to her knees as the cube-shaped bomb slowly rose from the deep pit and disappeared into the black void covering the hole of the torus.

Another black streak appeared from ground to sky, and the image of the torus blurred. The bottom edge of the pillar shot up and vanished far above.

The torus was gone.

The rest of Kate's energy flooded out of her. She sat on the dusty ground, breathing hard, too tired to cry.

Colonel Brighton knelt next to her. He rested his hand on her shoulder.

"We have to try something else," she said hoarsely.

He shook his head. "There is nothing else. All we can do now is prepare."

26

JEFF

Erikson was the first to speak over the comm line, his voice boiling with agitation.

"We can't leave! We've barely started our calculations—"

"The comet is *here!*" Jeff interrupted. "You have to get off the station!"

He unstrapped his safety harness and pulled himself toward the airlock of the *Seeker*. The door swung open and he floated into Venus Lab. Sandra floated within the spherical room, struggling to pull on her compression suit.

"Just bring it!" Jeff shouted.

He peeled the other two suits off the wall and grabbed the helmets. Without looking behind him, he pushed them toward the open door leading to the *Seeker*.

"Where are the other two?"

"I'll get them," Sandra said.

Jeff pushed past her, into the station. "You stay in the ship. Get ready to detach." He saw Erikson, still at his workstation. "What's the hold-up?!"

"The data!" said Erikson. "We haven't been able to send it back to Earth!"

The lights in the corridor blinked off and on. A slow vibration rattled the equipment bolted to the walls.

Jeff grabbed a handhold and pulled himself forward. He grabbed Erikson by the arms and kicked off the wall, flying back toward the airlock.

"We'll lose it all!" shouted Erikson in protest.

Hideo was still in his supply room at the end of the corridor, hurriedly trying to detach his laptop from its workstation.

"Time to leave, Hideo!" Jeff yelled at him.

Hideo nodded and yanked on the laptop. It ripped free, sending shiny bolts spinning slowly across the room.

Erikson had seemingly resigned himself to losing the data. He allowed Jeff to pull him through the open airlock and into the *Seeker*.

Sandra had strapped herself into the command chair. Her hands flew over the control panel.

A strong blue light bloomed outside the cockpit window.

"How're we looking?" Jeff asked, breathless.

"It's gonna be close," Sandra replied.

Jeff went back to the airlock. Hideo appeared on the other side, laptop in hand. Just as he was about to enter the airlock, he stopped.

"Wait!" he said.

He went back into the station.

"Hideo!" Jeff yelled.

The airlock door swung shut automatically, sealing Hideo inside Venus Lab.

"Sandra!"

"It wasn't me! It was the system!"

The ship lurched as it decoupled from the space station.

"Go back!" Jeff shouted.

"I can't! I'm locked out of the controls!"

"Oh, no," Erikson groaned.

Jeff kicked off the wall and smashed into a storage crate. He quickly pulled out his spacesuit.

"Niels, help me."

"It's too late."

"Help me!"

Erikson blinked and seemed to wake up. With shaking hands, he helped Jeff get into his spacesuit yet again.

"Sandra, he can open the airlock from inside, right?"

"As long as he has power."

Jeff pulled on his gloves and glanced out the cockpit window. The blue light steadily grew brighter.

"Spin the ship around after I'm out," Jeff told her. "Set the engine for a stage two burn. Keep your finger on the trigger. If something happens to us, get out."

She swallowed hard, then nodded.

Erikson handed Jeff his helmet.

"Thank you, Niels."

"Please save him," said Erikson.

Jeff pulled on his helmet and slid the neck lock into place. He waited inside the *Seeker*'s small airlock until it depressurized, then keyed in the command to open the door.

Blue light spilled into the airlock as the door rose, painting Jeff's boots, legs, then his torso. He lowered his sun visor as he drifted out of the airlock.

The space station was fifty meters away. Venus appeared blue behind it. Jeff let out a steady stream of nitrogen from his pack and coasted away from the *Seeker*.

"Hideo, if you can hear me, I'm coming to get you. Put your suit on."

Hideo grunted over the intercom. "Working on it. I'm sorry, Jeff."

A small blue comet shot past the station, and the lights inside flickered.

Jeff was twenty meters away.

"Get ready to open the airlock," said Jeff.

"I'm ready. As soon as you—"

A comet shot past Jeff and ripped through one end of the space station. Blue plasma smacked the hull like a paintball around the ragged hole. Shining metal debris tumbled away into space.

"Hideo!"

The lights in the station went dark. Venus Lab went into a slow spin.

"Jeffrey..." Sandra said from the *Seeker*, her voice filled with fear.

Jeff turned far enough to look back out of the corner of his eye.

A new planet had appeared behind the *Seeker*—a planet of pure blue energy.

The comet.

"Hideo?"

No response.

Jeff drifted closer to the spinning station. He only saw one way to get inside—through the hole the meteorite had just ripped in the hull.

And he only saw one way to get to it.

As he drifted closer, he readied the hook of his safety tether, unspooling a length of cable and holding the hook out in front of him.

The damaged portion of the station swung in front of him as he approached. He pushed his control stick and shot forward. The undamaged end of Venus Lab crashed into him on its spin like a bat hitting a baseball.

Jeff's sun visor slammed against the hull, cracking it down the middle.

The station's spin pulled him along the hull, toward the end. He felt like a lizard trying to hold on to the windshield of a speeding car. The hook of his safety tether scraped over the hull.

Jeff thrashed wildly, trying to grab onto something to stop his inexorable slide.

Light from the comet pierced through his cracked sun visor, and he howled in pain and frustration.

Jeff's legs drifted past the edge of the station.

The hook caught.

And held.

He was on the end of the station opposite the damage, but at least he had a lifeline. Hand over hand, he climbed across the hull, his safety tether extending behind him. The spin of the station gave him a view of Venus, then the comet—a constantly-changing vista of different shades of blue.

Jeff tried his best to avoid the glowing blue goop on the hull. The goop had spread out into a root-like network of tendrils that now covered nearly half the station. It seemed to pulse with a life of its own.

He reached the edge of the jagged hole and pulled himself inside Venus Lab.

"Hideo?"

The corridor was dark except for a patch of blue light spilling in from the small observation window. At the edge of the light, Hideo floated. Jeff drifted over to him and spun him around until they were face-to-face.

"Did you find him?" Erikson asked.

Jeff tapped a command on his wristpad and light on his helmet flicked on. Hideo was unconscious inside his suit...or worse. Jeff tapped on Hideo's wristpad, but it had shorted out.

"His system's down!" said Jeff. "He needs air. Coming back now."

He kicked off the wall and floated back to the hole, bringing Hideo with him.

"Jeff, I have to move the ship," said Sandra.

"I know! We're almost there."

"I have to move it now."

"One more minute."

"We don't have a minute!"

Jeff slammed against the inner wall of the station. With fumbling, gloved hands, he tied a knot in his safety line. Then he snapped Hideo's safety hook to the loop. Jeff drifted up through the hole and pulled Hideo up after him by his tether.

"There must be thousands of them," said Erikson.

Jeff looked up. The space around Venus was filled with countless blue meteorites. Debris from the larger comet had become a meteor shower that now rained down on Venus. Blue streaks of plasma punctured the cloudy atmosphere.

"We're coming back now," said Jeff.

He pulled Hideo close and prepared to kick off the hull of Venus Lab.

A meteorite hit the station next to him, breaking it in half and launching him sideways. Hideo slipped from his grasp as they tumbled away from each other, hurtling through space.

Jeff's safety line attached to the hull snapped taut, jerking him to a dead stop. He swung away from the station in a wide arc, like a pendulum.

Hideo drifted away quickly. His tether reached the end of its line and snapped fifty meters from Jeff. The jerking movement from the snapping tether slowed his drift, but he was still moving toward the incoming comet...and also the *Seeker*.

Jeff was still tethered to the spinning space station.

"I..." said Sandra over the intercom. "Jeff, I..."

"Grab Hideo," he said. "Then get out."

"But what about—"

"No discussion! You're going to lose power any second if you stay."

Another meteorite struck the half of Venus Lab to which Jeff was attached. It pushed the station farther away from the *Seeker*, carrying Jeff with it. He pawed at the tether controls near his waist, then twisted a dial and punched a button. The tether popped free.

Jeff maneuvered away from Venus Lab, short streams of nitrogen spurting from his pack. He managed to stabilize his tumble enough to face the *Seeker*, two hundred meters away. Hideo disappeared into the airlock.

Then the ship turned toward Jeff.

He thumbed his control stick in reverse and moved back, farther away from the ship.

"What are you doing?" Sandra asked.

"I told you to leave."

"No!"

"I have six hours of air left in this suit," said Jeff. "After the comet passes, you can come back and get me."

"It's not going to 'pass you', Mr. Dolan," said Erikson. "It's going to atomize you."

"Sandra," Jeff said, "if I don't see you turn that ship around right now, I will program my suit to drop me into the atmosphere. We don't have time for this!"

After a long moment, the nose of the ship swung away from him. Small orbital thrusters on the hull fired, pushing the ship out of the path of the comet. Light bloomed from the engine wash shield at the back of the craft as Sandra initiated a stage two burn.

Soon, the *Seeker* was no more than a speck in the distance.

Atta girl, Jeff thought.

A dozen meteorites passed through the area in space the *Seeker* had just occupied. The ship would have been ripped to shreds.

Jeff spun in place, then maneuvered parallel to the planet below, drifting away from the path of the incoming comet.

Deep down, he doubted if the small distance he could put between himself and its path would make any difference.

Not much else to do out here, he thought.

The crack in his sun visor glowed with the intensity of a cutting torch. His face tingled with uncomfortable warmth. Jeff had the terrifying thought of being cooked alive within his suit.

He spun around until he was traveling backward, spurting nitrogen now from the waist of his suit.

"Jeff," said Erikson. "You remember what happened last time your suit lost power. You barely survived."

"I remember."

Sandra's voice came on the line. "We won't be able to get you in time."

"Well, let's hope I don't lose power. Are you three okay?"

"Hideo is stable. I believe we're a safe distance away, though the lights keep flick—"

The line went dead.

Jeff glanced at his wristpad. His suit still had power. He slowed his drift until he was stationary.

A good a spot as any, he thought.

The comet rapidly grew in apparent size as it approached Venus. Its electric blue trail extended for thousands of miles into the distance. A million meteorites preceded its arrival, peppering the clouds of Venus like a handful of tiny pebbles thrown into a lake.

The HUD in Jeff's helmet flickered and went blank. He glanced at his wristpad. His system was down.

A vibration grew in his bones. He held his gloved hands in front of him. They were shaking so rapidly their edges were a blur.

The clouds over Venus parted as the comet breached the atmosphere, revealing a surface crawling with activity. There was no time to register any of it. The comet hit the surface, and the planet shook.

The cloud layer continued to peel back as a blue dome of plasma swelled up from the impact site, rapidly growing until it would have been large enough to cover the African continent on Earth.

Then it burst like a bubble, sending out a blue shockwave that demolished a good part of the working machinery on the surface.

Jeff watched as the cloud layer slowly crept back over the planet after its retreat, concealing the activity below.

And then it was over.

Jeff squeezed his hands into loose fists as the first sensation of cold crept in.

An object appeared in the distance, growing larger each second.

The alien.

Jeff was still orbiting the planet, but the creature maintained the same position as when Jeff first arrived at Venus Lab—waiting for its new home to become habitable.

If it's directly in my path, I'll splat into it like a bug, he thought morbidly.

He passed several hundred meters above it, reaching out for it with his thoughts.

One of those thoughts brushed the creature's mind. Jeff could feel it like a hum of electricity coursing through his veins—but he also felt the danger. Beneath the almost-pleasant sensation of connecting with the alien's mind lay a twisted thread of raw power. It was a cosmic live-wire snaking like an artery throughout all existence—a thing not meant to be experienced by any human.

Jeff reached for this thread and slammed to a stop in orbit as if hitting an invisible wall, his precious air crushed from his lungs. He hung suspended like a fly in amber, not only stuck in place but every inch of him frozen.

Below, between himself and Venus, the creature turned.

He tried to speak so he could say he was sorry for any transgression, but all that escaped his locked jaw was a pitiful groan. He tried to say it with his mind, but that door was closed.

There had been no malice in whatever action froze him in place. Jeff had sensed no anger during the millisecond his mind occupied the same space as the creature's.

Yet, as it slowly approached him, its bulk growing larger against the backdrop of a slowly-rotating Venus, Jeff struggled to think of a scenario that didn't result in his own painful death.

Looking at the massive creature head-on, Jeff was smaller than a guppy facing down an approaching megalodon. Its "mouth" was a glowing lava-colored oval slightly recessed into its rocky flesh. This pool of vibrant red light intensified as the alien drew closer, who was still helplessly frozen in place, forced to watch the alien's approach with wide and unblinking eyes.

Dark shapes moved in the creature's monstrous red mouth, bubbling just under the surface like a knot of eels.

The shapes coalesced into a circle, and a torus emerged from the alien's mouth, its black surface metal glowing red-hot.

Jeff's scream came out a quiet whisper as the torus overtook him, pulling him into its void-black center.

27

KATE

In the small room, Kate gently tugged on the fresh bandage wrapped around Santi's head, nudging it down to fully cover the cut on his temple. The cut on her own arm wasn't deep enough for stitches, so the nurse had tossed her some gauze and a role of medical tape as she rushed out the door to help another patient.

The nurses at the Namibian Defense Force naval base were competent but overworked, pushing through their exhaustion, operating mostly on a triage system that prioritized the many gravely wounded scientists and military personnel that were brought in from the comet impact site.

With a quick phone call, Colonel Brighton had arranged a helicopter for himself, Kate, Santi, and Neesha. It carried them 1000 kilometers north of the impact site, to the west coast of Namibia. The naval base overlooked the Atlantic Ocean—a view which Kate would otherwise have considered beautiful if it weren't for the steady rain of meteors plunging into the choppy surface.

Riley and the crew of the *Odyssey* had been somewhat successful, she had learned. While they managed to break apart the large comet that was on a collision course with Earth, they had shattered it into countless smaller projectiles.

Mercury was not so lucky. The comet intended for the closest planet to the Sun suffered the full brunt of an impact, leaving behind a crater the size of Australia and a haze of blue atmosphere that seemed to thicken by the minute.

Kate rubbed the tip of her thumb against the chromium ring Jeff had given her. There had been no word yet from Venus Lab, or from the *Odyssey*, regarding anything that happened after she sent her last message.

Santi slept peacefully despite his broken wrist, in no small part due to the pain medication the nurses had given him. Kate sighed and patted his uninjured arm. She stood and stretched with a groan. The adrenaline that had kept her moving for the past ten hours had all but fled her system, leaving behind aching muscles and a desire to sleep for several days without interruption.

A painting on the bare concrete wall of the small room depicted a fisherman on the coast, hauling in a net overflowing with his catch.

There were no windows in this section of the base. Everyone had been evacuated to the reinforced underground bunker two kilometers inland. It was connected to the coastal base by three long, descending tunnels wide enough for supply trucks.

Kate rubbed her eyes.

"How's he doing?" Neesha asked from the doorway.

A bandage covered her left upper arm where the nurses had removed a deep wood splinter. Other than that and a few light cuts on her cheek, she was in good shape.

"He'll be fine," Kate replied. "He woke up for a minute earlier and asked when he could go back to school." She hesitated before asking her next question. "What's it like up there?"

Neesha shrugged. "Well, you know how much I hate being dramatic..."

Kate offered a tired, knowing smile.

"It's downright apocalyptic," said Neesha. "I can't think of another way to put it."

Right on cue, the lights in the small room flickered. A deep, hollow *thoommmm* echoed in the distance. The two of them shielded their eyes as concrete dust showered down from the ceiling.

"Go take a look," said Neesha. "If this is it, you should at least see it coming."

Kate glanced down at Santi. "I don't want to leave him alone."

Neesha sat next to him and held his hand. "I'll stay. I've seen enough already."

Kate lingered. Finally, she said, "Thank you for everything, Neesh."

Neesha smiled. "Thank you for everything, too."

Santi's room was one of many lining a long concrete hallway in the underground section of the base. Lightbulbs hung from hooks on the ceiling.

Another meteor struck the base aboveground, shaking the walls. The ceiling lights dimmed for a long moment, then slowly brightened.

At the end of the hallway, Kate climbed a metal ladder that led her up to the top level of the bunker.

A soldier from the Namibian Defense Force nodded a greeting and helped her climb off the ladder. Her legs were shaking from the climb.

The sole room at the top of the underground bunker was a circular command center—a smaller version of the main command center at the primary facility. A ring of screens covered the walls. Three concentric circles of workstations faced the screens, with a command station at their heart.

Colonel Brighton and a group of military personnel Kate didn't recognize stood in the middle of the room at the command station, speaking quietly and occasionally pointing at the screens.

All of them showed the same image, albeit from different locations around the side of the planet unlucky enough to be facing the direction of the oncoming comets: blue meteor streaks falling from the sky, striking oceans, lakes, rivers, farmland, highways…and cities.

Colonel Brighton checked his watch, then noticed Kate standing off to the side, her arms folded over her chest as she watched the screens. He excused himself from his group and walked over to her.

"How much longer will it last?" she asked.

"An hour," Brighton replied. "Probably. The comet that the Odyssey crew broke apart was larger than we thought. It created a substantial amount of debris. Some of it is going right past us, but the rest…"

He gestured at the screens.

"It's horrible," said Kate.

"A degree of horrible less than the alternative," he added, "but horrible nonetheless."

"What about Venus?"

"Confirmed impact, same as Mercury," said Brighton.

Kate watched a live feed of Newport Beach, California. Two meteors hit the shore in rapid succession, sending a wall of water over a neighborhood of houses.

"We evacuated as many as possible," said the Colonel. "Hard to send them to a safe location when everywhere is a target. I can't help but wonder if there was another way to stop it."

"We did what we could," said Kate.

The Colonel frowned. "Before the mission to destroy the comet, some of my colleagues at the Pentagon were prepping the Odyssey for something else."

Kate thought about it a moment. "That explains why it was ready to go so quickly."

Brighton nodded. "I commandeered the vessel when I realized what we were up against. My colleagues had decided we should capture the alien for study. They bolted a tensor net system onto the front of the Odyssey to haul the creature back to Earth orbit."

Kate's eyes widened. "The orbital shipyards."

"Yes," Brighton admitted. "One of the six was to be used to house the alien."

She cackled with laughter, unable to control herself. "No wonder the contracts went through so quickly! Neesha warned me to be careful when I signed them."

"I'm telling you because I can't fight the administration anymore," said Brighton. "Whether it happens next year or in the next fifty, my colleagues will try again. They won't forget the alien is out there."

Kate wiped her eyes as she settled down, then sighed heavily as crushing drowsiness seeped into her bones.

"Have you heard from Jeff?" she asked.

"No. I'm sorry. Carol is still on board the Odyssey. She had planned to swing by the lab on her way back to check for..." he paused a moment before adding, "...survivors."

Kate turned toward him. "Just Carol? What about the others?"

Brighton shook his head.

A wave of dizziness washed over Kate and she stumbled in place. Brighton grabbed her elbow and guided her into a chair as she collapsed.

"You need rest," he told her.

"I need to watch," she whispered.

An image lingered on the aftermath of a meteor impact in the middle of a populated European city. Buildings crumbled around the crater. Glowing blue plasma covered the area like webbing.

"We'll survive," said Brighton, staring at the same screen. "Everything is going to change, but we'll survive."

Kate sat silently, hands held loosely in her lap, and watched the meteors fall, and fall, and fall.

28

JEFF

Captain Jeff Dolan of the *Sojourner* snapped awake in his chair, a quick shout escaping his lips. The other five members of his bridge crew turned in their seats to look at him, concern on their faces.

"Are you alright, Captain?" asked a woman standing at his side.

Jeff looked up at her—short hair, intelligent eyes, dark uniform—then down at his hands, turning them over slowly, rubbing his fingertips. He had been daydreaming about Venus and must have drifted off.

"Captain?" the woman prompted.

He realized he knew her name.

"Thank you, Commander Reyes," he said with a dry throat, shifting in his chair. "I'm fine."

Reyes met the eyes of each member of the bridge crew. "Back to work then."

Reluctantly, they turned to face their stations.

Jeff took in the bridge as if seeing it for the first time. His chair was the centerpiece of a square room with a peaked ceiling—almost pyramidal in shape but for the small white sphere at the apex. The sphere turned slowly, casting a warm white glow to every corner.

A large view screen dominated the front of the room, showing a rapidly-enlarging blue planet against a backdrop of stars.

Crew stations were spaced along the walls of the bridge. Jeff glanced over the people seated at each one and rattled off their names in his head as if he'd known them his entire career: Lassiter, Xian, Crosier, Amoaku, and Reinholdt.

His commander, Julia Reyes, checked her wristpad and clasped her hands behind her back as she stared at the approaching planet on the view screen. Jeff looked down at her black shoes, a strange thought tickling his mind.

Gravity. She wasn't floating free.

He studied the view screen, less interested in the blue planet toward which his ship was speeding than the image itself. The screen wasn't rotating, which meant that the camera was either compensating for the spin of a centrifuge—or there was no centrifuge, and the ship was making its gravity a different way. Yet, to add to his mounting confusion, he couldn't think of the method.

Jeff rubbed his eyes hard to try and clear his thoughts. There was a thick fog in his mind that he couldn't penetrate—not completely unlike being hungover.

"Did we celebrate last night?" he quietly asked Reyes.

She leaned toward him, a slight frown creasing her lips. "Captain?"

"Did we drink?"

"No, sir. Just another long work day prepping for

the rendezvous."

He nodded and studied the view screen. The blue planet was a glowing billiards ball in a sea of black. A single white strip of atmosphere banded its equator.

I know this mission, Jeff thought. *I know everything about why I'm here and what I'm supposed to do.*

He tried to remember anything before the mission—before the *Sojourner* had launched from the orbital shipyard near Earth where it was built—but every time he got close enough to reach for the shape of a memory, it slipped through his fingers and vanished into the fog.

"Are we prepared to dock?" he asked, watching a stream of data scroll up the right side of the view screen.

Crosier, his aging comms officer, turned in his seat. "I've relayed our Luna-class specs to the Wisdom's crew. I've been assured the airlocks will be compatible."

"Xian, slow us down," said Jeff.

A woman with long black hair sitting to the left of the screen slid her hands over the surface of her workstation, tapping commands faster than the eye could register. The *Sojourner*'s main engine cut out.

"Braking maneuver engaged," said Xian, her voice monotone.

Jeff stood, smoothing down the front of his uniform. He frowned at it, noting the shining Diamond Aerospace insignia on the left shoulder.

"There's no need to drag this out," he addressed the crew. "After we dock with the Wisdom, Commander Reyes and Dr. Lassiter will go aboard to secure the information." He looked at each of them in turn. "The captain of the Wisdom knows what's at stake just as much as we do. With Earth's defenses compromised, we might be the last hope for turning the tide back home. We cannot fail."

He sat down in his chair and pulled up the *Sojourner*'s schematics on his palm reader. It was a hybrid vessel, designed for speed and deep scanning, with a modest arsenal of light artillery should it meet the opposition. Its small caliber guns wouldn't be enough to punch through the hull of a warship, but they could algorithmically target surface guns and scanners while the *Sojourner* made its escape.

At its core, the ship was a simple cube—the original *Luna* design, constructed to accept modular attachments that would fit any purpose.

Jeff thought he knew the person who spearheaded the team that brought the now-ubiquitous *Luna* design to life, but he couldn't remember her name to save his life. It felt like a long time ago.

"I'm getting something from the Wisdom," said Crosier. "Audio only."

Jeff leaned forward in his seat. "Let's hear it."

Static burst over the bridge speakers, then quieted as Crosier slid a control on his panel.

"—some kind of signal bombardment from a surface installation," said a beleaguered voice. Warning klaxons blared in the background. "It's preventing us from broadcasting the data. We didn't know they had a station down there."

There was a loud rumble and the signal cut out.

"How long until we get to them?" Jeff asked.

Xian's graceful hands flew over her console. "Coming into visual range."

The blue planet filled the view screen, painting the bridge in vivid hues. A gray smudge marred the white strip of atmosphere across the planet's middle—the *Wisdom.* The freighter had been waiting for the *Sojourner* under the guise of a transport siphoning trace gases from the blue planet's exosphere.

The audio signal burst through the speakers.

"—something embedded in the signal. Malicious code. We've lost control of the ship. The fires…oh God the fires…"

"Get us there, Xian," Jeff urged.

"Captain, we can't dock if they're on fire," said Reyes at his side.

"We need to evacuate the Wisdom. If they can't broadcast the data, we have to get it out ourselves."

"I've located the foreign signal," said Crosier. "It's a tight-band from the surface, focused directly on the Wisdom. If they broaden their stream, it will hit us, too."

"We'd be trapped," Reyes growled.

Jeff chewed his thumbnail, his eyes desperately scanning the view screen. He pushed himself to his feet and stepped toward the screen.

"Mr. Crosier, a line to the Wisdom."

The comms officer tapped a screen on his console. "Open."

"Captain Brand, this is Captain Jeff Dolan of the Sojourner."

A crackle of static over the intercom, then: "Don't come near this place. The Wisdom is breaking apart."

"Captain, if the signal were interrupted, could you send a data packet back to Earth?"

"We can't get anything past our own hull—"

"Do you have the *capability?*" Jeff interrupted.

"We just have long-range comms and life support, and they're hanging by a thread."

"Xian," Jeff said, rushing to the navigation officer's workstation. She looked up at him with silver irises. Half her face was etched with a flesh-colored matrix of thin, intricate wiring. "Maintain our speed until the last second. Swing us around the backside of the Wisdom. Put us directly between them and the planet."

"It will be a rough ride," she told him, her hands already working the controls.

"That's why we have seatbelts," Jeff muttered under his breath as he jogged back to his chair.

"You know what this means," Reyes said into his ear as Jeff buckled his safety harness.

He paused and met her eye. "No more late-night celebrations."

A hint of a smile tugged at her lips.

"Everyone strap in!" Reyes shouted as she found her own chair and secured her safety harness.

"Don't hold back, Xian," said Jeff. "We can't give the surface installation a chance to widen the signal. Still there, Captain Brand?"

"I think I know what you're up to."

"I need you to send that data toward Earth as soon as the Sojourner blocks the surface signal. Single burst."

"I'm ready."

"Swinging around," said Xian.

The blue planet lunged sideways on the view screen. Jeff's stomach slid with it. Xian worked her controls and the *Sojourner* leveled out, aimed straight at the *Wisdom*. For being a freighter, she was only several times larger than the *Sojourner*—a fact that worked to the plan's advantage. Jeff supposed Captain Brand had ditched the ship's freight containers to make himself a smaller target.

The *Wisdom* swept across the star field on the view screen and out of sight.

"Hold on," said Xian.

Atmospheric boosters fired and the crew slammed forward against their harnesses, all of them crying out in pain. Jeff's vision dimmed as his eyeballs swelled in their sockets.

The pressure eased and he slumped back into his seat.

Xian tapped a red warning box on her control panel. "In position."

"Good work," said Jeff, breathing hard.

Crosier's console exploded with activity. He leaned back in surprise as warning signals flooded his screens. Control schema with foreign writing flashed and vanished faster than he could touch them.

A high-pitched squeal pierced the speakers, then went silent. All the consoles on the bridge lit up yellow and blinked out.

"Navigation offline," said Xian.

"*Everything* offline," Reyes added, checking her dead console.

A distant siren blared from another part of the ship.

"Fire," Jeff whispered.

A deep explosion rocked the bridge.

In the silence that followed, the speakers crackled.

"Sojourner, this is Wisdom. Packet sent. It's done."

"Thank you, Captain."

"I've some bad news."

"Don't hold back on our account."

"They've taken control of our weapon system, even with you blocking the signal. My operations officer informed me that we're about to fire on your vessel."

Jeff unbuckled his safety harness and approached the view screen. The *Wisdom* spun slowly, adrift. Jagged holes punctured its hull, the charred metal peeling outward.

The front of the ship swung around, and two flashes of orange light blipped into and out of existence.

The first missile hit the *Sojourner*'s port side engine, shearing it away in a confetti burst of shredded plating. The second hit dead-center, piercing the bridge.

Jeff screamed as the view screen exploded toward him, the debris behind it propelled through his rag-doll body by a blooming wall of fire.

29

JEFF

He awoke with a gasp, his hands grabbing at the ribbons of his chest—only he was whole again. Jeff looked down at his gray engineer's coveralls in a panic, unable to make sense of the transition. Milliseconds earlier he had felt his body separate— felt himself come apart.

He sat in a transparent chair at a transparent polycarbonate table. A second chair sat empty on the opposite side. The room's glossy, dark blue walls met at a point far above the table, forming a pyramid shape similar to the bridge aboard the *Sojourner*.

The image of a ship called *Wisdom* drifting in orbit of a bright blue planet flashed through Jeff's mind like a fresh dream upon waking. Inside the dream, Jeff couldn't remember Kate or anything else about his past—he only knew the mission.

I was a captain, Jeff thought.

He tried to hold on to the memory so he could pick it apart—but, like a dream, it began to fade.

Already he was having trouble remembering the details.

The hard floor in the pyramid-shaped room warmed the soles of his bare feet. A small white sphere turned at the apex, just as one had on the ship. Thin trails of soft blue light pulsed up the tiled walls toward the sphere.

There was no entrance to the room, and Jeff was alone.

He stood hesitantly, his chair sliding back without a sound. He half-expected something or someone to stop him. When no one did, he walked to the wall and leaned in close to a thin stream of light. His finger disappeared up to the second knuckle, and when he pulled it out, a faint blue glow clung to his skin.

"Hello?" he said loudly, rubbing at the glow on his finger.

He stared at the empty chair opposite the one in which he'd just been sitting. No door in the room, yet two chairs.

Jeff closed his eyes and attempted to regain his focus.

And then he felt it.

The room was stacked using fold space. There were hundreds of versions, one atop the other, identical in composition—but perhaps not in content.

Jeff mentally accessed the small black sphere the tori had implanted in his brain when they returned him to Earth after his first mission to Titan—the gift that allowed him to navigate fold space.

To his naked eye, nothing changed. Yet in his mind he could sense himself cycling through the same room—traveling the stack of identical versions. More than hundreds, as he first thought—*thousands*. Someone had stacked the same room thousands of times.

Why? he wondered. *Not for storage. It's empty.*

A man blinked into existence in the second empty chair and vanished just as quickly. Jeff cycled back through the rooms he'd already visited until the man popped into being once again.

He wore a long coat which spilled over the sides of his transparent chair. A lightweight armored vest covered a thermal shirt, which was tucked into faded black combat pants.

Short silver hair hugged his scalp, which was itself criss-crossed with a dozen white scars. One of those scars trailed down his forehead and over his left eye, the pupil of which was a milky white. He clenched his fists on the table. His left hand was made of metal.

"Well done, Jeffrey," said the man, smiling sadly.

Jeff exhaled as if he'd been punched by the sound of the man's voice.

"You—" he said hoarsely, unable to finish the sentence. He stumbled to his chair and collapsed into it.

"No," the man replied. "*You.*"

It was him. It was Jeffrey Dolan staring from across the table—slightly older, undeniably more weathered, but it was himself.

"You…" said the younger Jeff, trying it once again. "You've looked better."

The older Jeff burst out laughing, his rough voice booming against the hard walls and floor. His laughter tapered off into a grin.

"Thank you for that. I haven't laughed in ages. Of course, I could always count on me to laugh at my own jokes."

"Kate helps a lot with that, too."

The older man's smile faded. "Yes," he said quietly. "Yes, she did."

The silence stretched into uncomfortable territory.

"Are you really me?" Jeff asked.

The older version of himself nodded. "I'm really you. Though you can think of me as the Envoy if that makes it easier. It's the only name I've known for a long, long time."

"What is this?" Jeff asked, gesturing to the room.

The Envoy glanced around. "This? This is just a room."

"And the ship? Was I dreaming?"

"Not a dream. A test."

"But *this* is real."

"Extremely."

Jeff crossed his arms. "Did I pass the test?"

The older man spread his fingers out on the table—half of them real, half metal. "Well...you're here."

Jeff shifted in his seat as an unpleasant thought occurred to him.

"What would have happened if I failed?"

The Envoy tapped a metal finger on the polycarbonate table. "The Weaver found you in orbit, correct?"

"Weaver?"

"The alien. The big thing up there." He pointed at

the ceiling, then snapped his metal fingers. "Oh, but that's right. You haven't created its name yet."

Jeff squinted. "Are you from the future?"

"Are you from the past?"

"So I *don't* die in my suit above Venus. The…Weaver…saves me and I go on to become…" He waved his hand vaguely toward the older version of himself.

"*If* you pass the test."

"Didn't I already?"

"You passed the first one."

Jeff frowned. "How?"

"Earth got the data packet. Disaster averted."

"Does that really happen? I mean, in reality and not in a…simulation?"

The Envoy smiled. "You and I would need a lot more than a prosthetic arm if it really happened."

"So what is this, some kind of interview?"

"In a way."

Jeff leaned back in his chair. "Why me?"

"That's not for me to explain. Can we take a walk?"

"How? There's no—"

A line of vertical light split the wall behind the Envoy. He stood as the line widened to become a door.

Jeff shouted in surprise to find himself suddenly inside an outdated bright orange Constellation-class Mark V spacesuit. He floated up out of his chair as gravity receded. The Envoy's boots remained firmly on the floor. Jeff could hear his voice clearly inside his helmet.

"Your pack is full."

Jeff pressed the suit's control stick under his left thumb and his pack spat nitrogen, propelling him over the table. He followed the Envoy into the rectangle of light filling the doorway...

...and out onto the surface of Venus.

A strong wind blew the collar of the Envoy's jacket as he squinted against the harshness of the yellow Sun beaming down through holes in the atmosphere. Yellow dust hung suspended all around, forming a loose layer of fog extending in every direction.

Jeff rotated to look back. The doorway—and any building it might have led from—had vanished.

"Why don't you need a suit?" he asked his older self, spinning back around. "Is that some kind of enhancement we get in the future?"

The Envoy chuckled, shaking his head. "No, humans still can't breathe in space. I don't need a suit because I'm not really here." He pointed toward the horizon. "This way."

He strode into the fog, hands clasped behind his back. Jeff coasted gently forward, keeping pace.

"If you're not here, then where are you?"

"Back in my time, doing Kem-knows-what. Probably having more fun than I am. No offense." He offered an apologetic half-grin. "I'm more of a mirror image of my real self—or, *your* real self. It can be confusing. Weavers don't view time and space the same way we do. Nor do they subscribe to our notion of what constitutes physical reality."

The fog began to clear, and Jeff saw into the vast distance.

Dark shapes tumbled in the lower atmosphere,

larger than any skyscraper. Blue lightning arced between them, silhouetting their massive bulk.

"The machines work fast," the Envoy explained. "Pressure, atmosphere...gravity. There's just as much going on beneath us as there is above."

Jeff had witnessed a similar operation on Titan as he plummeted toward the icy surface at the end of his first mission—similar in design but not in scope. The operation on Titan had been isolated; confined to a few square miles with the purpose of bringing a member of the Weaver's race back from extinction.

What he saw on Titan paled in comparison to what he now witnessed. This was global. This was terraforming—the changing of a world to make it livable for a new inhabitant.

Toward that singular end, the surface of Venus crawled with activity.

Rivers of inky liquid cut the landscape, flowing between rising cities comprised of jet black geometric structures. Innumerable tori drifted between the sites, most of them funneling viscous liquid from the rivers into the voids within their rings. Above the city-sites, multifaceted structures emerged from the mouths of enormous tori in pieces or in whole, ferried down to the surface by a legion of humanoid drones in identical bright orange spacesuits.

"The Weaver still hasn't found a more adept working machine than the human body," said the Envoy.

"That's unfortunate," Jeff said grimly.

He watched as a six-sided skyscraper erupted from the ground not a hundred meters before him and rose slowly toward the pale yellow sky.

"Not really," the Envoy replied. "The tori only needed a few of us to get the blueprint down. Now it can make us *ad infinitum* without killing anyone else." He shrugged. "Seems like a great deal to me."

"Not for the ones it killed."

The Envoy regarded his younger self for a long moment. "I keep forgetting..."

"Forgetting what?"

The older man turned away and started walking. "That you're not me. Not yet."

"Do I ever not care that people die?" asked Jeff, his pack spitting nitrogen to propel him forward.

"Later, when your decisions must be based on species instead of communities...perhaps."

A drone drifted overhead and disappeared into the side of a torus. Heat distortions from the surface shimmered upward, causing Jeff to sweat in his spacesuit. The Envoy seemed unbothered by the temperature.

"Venus was already hot," he said, seeming to know Jeff's mind. He pointed to a wall of black smoke on the horizon. At one end of the wall, an active volcano belched debris into the sky. Behind it loomed the outlines of an entire range of volcanoes that dwarfed the first. "But not hot enough. The Weaver's planet was primordial. Oceans of lava that never cooled. A surface that was constantly remade as continuous eruptions altered the landscape. Not to mention a far more powerful sun. It will be the same here."

The Envoy directed Jeff's attention to the opposite horizon. In the distance, a thick pillar of white smoke rose into the sky, disappearing against the pockmarked yellow atmosphere that had—until recently—wholly smothered the surface of Venus. At the base of the pillar of white smoke sprawled a massive black pyramid, its edges glowing with piercing blue light.

The Envoy made straight for it, picking up his pace. Jeff thumbed his control stick, his pack streaming nitrogen to keep up.

"The Weavers are symbiotic," said the Envoy. "They do fine on their own, but they only thrive when they form a positive relationship with other species. One such relationship grants them a unique perspective on the definitions of space and time, which is how I'm standing here. Other relationships have a more straightforward benefit, like the one that allows entire planets to be remade."

"The Weaver isn't doing this?" Jeff asked, nodding toward a dozen drones as they floated past.

"It has a directive, which is to alter Venus." The Envoy took a moment to gather his thoughts. "Some symbiotic relationships are equally beneficial, and others benefit one side to an unfair advantage. The Weaver needs an arbiter of change that can remake entire worlds. Its own goals would otherwise be impossible to achieve. I would describe its chosen arbiter as...dominant."

Jeff kept his eyes on the black pyramid. It towered over all emerging machine cities spread across the surrounding miles.

"Is this a test to see if the Weaver can be symbiotic with humans?" Jeff asked.

"Not with all of them."

"Me? I mean, us?"

"There is no me without you," said the Envoy. "If you don't make it off Venus, I can't guess what would happen to me." He nodded toward the pyramid. "But I do know that what's behind those doors...the arbiter of change that I mentioned...it has no use for anything that doesn't further its purpose."

The base of the pyramid covered at least a half-mile of ground. A dozen deep steps led to a pair of obsidian doors ten stories high. After the Envoy climbed the last stair, Jeff's suit brought him down to the ground as gravity returned. He and the Envoy stood before the closed doors like ants before the hall of a giant.

"Do I have to do this?" Jeff asked.

"If you want the chance to see Kate again, yes. It's a small chance, but better than nothing." The Envoy glanced around. "Besides, where else would you go?"

He reached for Jeff and, without warning, took off his spacesuit helmet and tossed it aside.

"You can breathe now," he said before Jeff could protest having his helmet pulled away. "When you go in there, try not to worry about dying. You were going to do that anyway and it will only cloud your judgement."

"Imminent death tends to do that." Jeff peeled off his gloves and let them fall to the ground. "You're not coming inside?"

He slapped Jeff on the shoulder and started back down the stairs. "I've already been. Besides, I have faith in us."

"Hey," said Jeff. The Envoy turned. "How do we lose the arm?"

The older version of himself smiled. "In the best way possible."

He gave a little salute and turned away.

30

JEFF

Jeff reached for the doors. They appeared to be constructed from the same light-swallowing material as the exterior of the tori.

The doors opened without a touch, swinging silently inward—what must have been thousands upon thousands of tons gliding as if the slightest breath could set them in motion.

Jeff walked into the pyramid. The floor and walls were a grid of large, glossy black tiles five meters to a side. With a quick glance from side to side just beyond the massive doors, Jeff estimated there were at least forty tiles.

Soft blue light flowed like lazy streams between the tiles, creating a glowing wireframe pyramid across the five interior surfaces.

The palatial structure was empty but for a tiled ziggurat in the middle of the floor, a hundred meters from the doors. Each of its five stepped levels was twice as tall as Jeff. A wide transparent tube emerged from the topmost level and rose to the apex of the pyramid. Thick fog swirled violently within, gradating from black at the bottom to ash gray in the middle, and then to white near the top, just before the tube passed through the roof.

Jeff walked forward slowly, his boots silent against the absorbent material of the black tiles.

He didn't hear the doors closing behind him, but he felt the air displacement. Turning back, he had the sudden urge to run—and then the doors swung all the way shut, concealing the swarm of activity outside.

Jeff took a deep breath and started walking.

He patted the pockets of his spacesuit, seeking anything that might help him if he were to be tested. Finding every pocket empty, Jeff swallowed hard, his throat bone dry. All of his hopes aside, after what he'd seen on the surface, after what he'd experienced because of the tori—what difference could be made with a trinket small enough to fit inside his pocket?

When he was halfway to the ziggurat, the swirling fog inside the tube darkened completely and froze solid, becoming a pillar of needle-thin charcoal crystals. Jeff stopped walking and held his breath. An energy that hadn't been in the room when he first entered was steadily building in the background.

He tapped into fold space to check if there were other versions of the pyramid interior stacked atop each other, and he screamed. His knees buckled and he dropped to the tile like a boneless fish. Jeff jammed his knuckles into his temples to stop the pressure and screamed louder as blood leaked from his nose and ears.

He had accessed an unfathomably powerful stream of energy flowing through the pyramid. It overloaded his brain, which swelled and sizzled inside the scorching confines of his skull.

It was pure unconscious instinct that allowed him to switch over to another version of the pyramid's interior and cut himself off from the energy stream.

He lay on the floor, gasping. His eyes burned; the blood that had leaked from his nose and ears was painfully hot, as was the tile beneath him. A drop of his blood hit the tile and began to smoke.

A whisper emerged from the wide tube rising from the ziggurat. The crystal pillar within softened; became less dense. It pushed through the tube wall and into the main pyramid chamber, floating as a dark mist over the tiles—toward Jeff.

He spat blood and strained to stand up as the mist approached. As it grew closer, its mote-like particles formed tiny shards of reflective glass-like material that glinted with blue light. It stopped halfway from the ziggurat, a ten-meter-tall cloud of gently spinning broken black glass.

Jeff wiped his nose and swayed in place, blinking hard as the pain from his mental encounter gradually subsided.

When the cloud of glass spoke, its voice was smooth as a velvet river; sonorous as a bell struck in a concert hall.

"I am called the Worldshaper."

Jeff blinked slowly, struggling to stay upright.

"My legacy is seen across the universe," continued the soothing, disembodied voice of the Worldshaper. "Will you ask my purpose?"

Jeff had to force the strained words out through a constricted throat. "I can guess." He closed his eyes as he spoke, the pressure in his skull mounting with every word. "Worldshaper. Doesn't leave much to the imagination."

A wave of movement swept down the cloud's glass-like particles, sending a band of reflected light from top to bottom.

"You are not unique," it told Jeff. "There have been thousands like you. There will be thousands more." A long moment of silence crawled by, then it added, "You are less than a blink in the eye of the universe."

Jeff took a deep, painful breath. "Then why am I here?"

The cloud of shards drifted closer—a tapestry of spinning glass catching blue light that flowed between the pyramid's black tiles. As the Worldshaper approached, the cloud changed its shape, forming into a rough approximation of a ten-meter-tall human figure that came to a stop in front of Jeff, hovering several meters off the floor.

When next it spoke, the Worldshaper's voice surrounded him like river water rushing around a boulder. The sound was electric honey poured into his ears and skull, and he staggered sideways with the sheer power of it.

"Physical worlds aren't the only ones that need shaping. If I fail to harvest a human connection, Earth must be reshaped until a suitable species emerges."

"Reshaped," Jeff whispered.

"As was Titan and its parent. As was Mars. As were planets you will name Galena and Meridian. Countless others."

"No new species emerged on Mars."

The human-shaped cloud of shards seemed to bend at the waist, its head lowering toward Jeff.

"None that you know of." It stood up straight. "As I said...less than a blink."

The humanoid shape dissolved into a faint cloud of smaller particles that swirled around Jeff like a slow-motion whirlpool. The diameter of the swirl steadily shrank as the particles drifted closer together.

"You will die when I return you to orbit," said the voice, now fully inside Jeff's mind. "Do you know this?"

Jeff's voice spoke without his mouth moving. "I know it."

The slow-moving swirl of particles tinkled like broken glass. The Worldshaper's voice was urgent now—entreating.

"I could save you. I could send you back to Earth, breathing and alive. Give me permission to reshape Earth in a thousand years and I will bring you home."

Jeff thought his next words and they spoke from within the mass of particles.

"Why do you need my permission?'

"I govern the shaping of worlds, but I am governed by the laws that shaped me. Your permission is required."

Jagged particles whispered against Jeff's cheeks and forehead. Blood trickled from the cuts. His limbs grew cold as he felt himself lifted from the floor.

He closed his eyes.

"You have thoughts about Kate," said the Worldshaper. "You can see her again."

An icy breeze touched Jeff's chest. He looked

down to see that his spacesuit was dissolving, tiny shreds of it disappearing into the swirling particles.

"You yourself have been reshaped," the voice continued. "Your return to Earth after dying on Titan was a glitch in the torus programming...a subroutine to ensure the existence of that which has not yet procreated. It was nothing more than nature's prime directive in binary form, carelessly engrained in the tori by their creators for their own benefit...yet it saved you from oblivion." The Worldshaper fully enshrouded Jeff in its particles until they formed a solid shell inches from his skin. The shell became a blur as its individual particles vibrated faster and faster. The Worldshaper's next words shook every bone in Jeff's body. *"Give me permission."*

Jeff had the knowledge that his skin was atomizing—pulling away like sand from his bones to merge with the cloud that was the Worldshaper. Yet it was a distant sensation—dulled as if it were happening to someone else.

His voice spoke just as loudly as the Worldshaper's.

"Put me back in orbit. I'm through with your tests."

A voice, growing more distant: "This wasn't the test."

Jeff's own words, traveling away with the other voice: "Then what is?"

A blast of yellow light stabbed his eyes like daggers and he cried out in pain.

The light dimmed and irised down to reveal a glowing yellow sphere against a never-ending wall of black: the Sun.

Jeff grabbed for his face but his gloved hands thumped against his helmet's face shield. He squeezed the fingers of his left hand through his glove with those of his right, knowing for certain his skin had been dissolved down to his bones inside the pyramid.

Yet he was once again whole.

He took a deep breath and laughed out loud. Tiny crystals fogged the inside of his face shield when he exhaled. Jeff frowned and checked his wristpad—blank screen.

The Worldshaper had put him back exactly where the Weaver had found him—in orbit around Venus and almost out of oxygen. Even now, he felt the strain on his lungs.

Jeff wondered if he had passed the test. He wondered if he even *wanted* to pass it. His mind swam with thoughts of Kate and the Envoy—of the future.

He craned his neck to search the darkness. The *Seeker* was nowhere to be found.

Long minutes passed. It became harder and harder to breathe. Time slowed. Jeff's eyelids drooped lower, and lower. The last thing he saw before his vision darkened was a blurry vision of Venus, its clouds passing beneath him, drifting toward change.

31

CAROL

The comet disappeared.

Commander Carol Brighton blinked in surprise. The piercing blue light that had been flooding through the narrow cockpit window from behind the ship flicked off.

Thirty seconds more and the *Odyssey* would have been overtaken by the comet. The ship shot forward, free from the invisible bindings that had been pulling it back.

"Riley?" she said. "Piper?"

Carol ran a diagnostic on the ship's systems. Everything was in the green. Her gloved hands flew over the console as she tried to diagnose the situation.

The star charts showed the *Odyssey* as being in the same region of space as it was moments before.

"So I've hardly moved..." Carol muttered, shaking her head.

Blue light flooded the cabin and every alarm in the *Odyssey* shrieked as the comet blinked back into existence—

—only this time it was in front of the ship.

The *Odyssey* rattled violently in the comet's wake as debris from the comet peppered its hull. Swirls of blue gas washed over the ship like neon aurorae.

Carol increased thrust and veered to port, clearing the turbulence.

One by one, the alarms went silent.

She forced the system through four rounds of diagnostics, just to be sure—paying particularly close attention to hull integrity.

So far, the *Odyssey* was still in one piece, thanks in no small part to Riley's patch of the hull.

She now had a clear view of the quickly-receding comet, and of its brilliant blue tail. The comet was already thousands and thousands of miles away—almost a mere spark in the distance once more.

"Commander Riley," said Carol, opening every comm frequency. "Piper. This is the Odyssey. Are you out there?"

Ship's scans weren't kicking back any signs of life in the vicinity. Carol triggered the *Odyssey*'s homing beacon—a signal the Constellation-class spacesuits could lock onto for pickup.

A small yellow rectangle popped up in the middle of her console.

She tapped it, and the rectangle expanded to an audio stream that danced as it relayed a message from her father, the Colonel.

"Carol, if you get this, that means you succeeded. Which also means I have a better chance of being here when you get back."

Carol smiled as warmth flooded her body. Tears pooled at the corners of her eyes. Not so long ago, she would have taken a two-year hauling mission to Mars to avoid hearing his voice so often.

"I need you to swing by Venus Lab on your way home. Dolan's ship is only big enough for two, so you may need to take on extra passengers. The Odyssey is fast enough to catch Venus before it's too far along its orbit for a rendezvous. In another three days, we won't be able to attempt any kind of rescue mission."

She programmed a full stop and set the system to perform the maneuvers on its own. The process would take a little over three hours, after which she could plot a course for Venus.

"Carol, be safe," said her father. "All my love."

The message ended.

She stared at the control panel.

Riley and Piper had been directly in the path of the comet, as had the Odyssey. If the ship had somehow escaped being overtaken, was there a chance they might have been spared as well?

Carol didn't want to admit the truth—that anyone outside the ship when the comet passed could not have survived.

She would leave the homing beacon on all the same.

Carol unbuckled her safety harness and looked toward the back of the ship.

Beyond the crew cabin, Sergeant Miller's boot was visible on the work table in the lab. The blue substance that infected him after the meteorite impacted the hull had crept over his spacesuit, cocooning him in a thick layer of fuzzy mold. Carol's gaze drifted up to the air vent above her head, wondering if any of the substance had gotten into the recirculation system.

Thinking back on the meteorite shower, she realized she'd have to warn her father that there was likely more of the blue substance on the hull of the *Odyssey*. Bringing it to the International Space Station would not make for a welcome return.

Carol drifted through the crew cabin and into the lab.

Keeping her distance from Miller's body, she searched through storage bins and cubbies until she found what she was looking for: a long roll of thick, clingy plastic wrap used for securing bundles of trash and human waste for jettisoning.

It took her half an hour to wrap Miller's body in plastic from head to toe on the table, encasing him like a mummy. She was thankful for zero gravity for a change. Being able to float around the table to wrap his body was much easier than trying to avoid the blue mold while reaching over him from a standing position.

Carol found a hand drill in Riley's tool bag. She removed the bolts that kept the work table legs secured to the floor. Miller's body and the table drifted free.

It was a tight fit, but she managed to maneuver the table through the crew cabin and into the airlock.

As Carol sealed the door between herself and the

table, she wondered if any of the blue substance had escaped her plastic mummification of Miller's body.

Guess I'll find out soon enough, she thought as she opened the outer airlock door.

Without pressurizing the airlock first, the table shot out of it like a bullet from a gun, carrying Miller's body into space.

Carol checked her wristpad—only thirty minutes before the ship came to a full stop. She bid Miller a silent farewell, gritting her teeth in anger at not being able to afford him the respect he deserved.

After running another fruitless scan for Riley and Piper, she spent the remaining time barricading the section of the lab where the meteorite had punched through. Traces of blue gunk still remained around the patch. If she was going to be welcoming new passengers, she didn't want them going anywhere near it.

The next forty-eight hours were filled with busywork. Carol checked and re-checked the ship's systems; verified oxygen levels and cleaned the scrubbers every few hours; re-plotted the *Odyssey's* current course multiple times to make sure she hadn't made a mistake.

She also said a proper farewell to Miller.

He had mostly kept to himself, even during the rare moments the crew really let down their collective guard. His unobtrusive personality only became glaringly obvious due to his absence.

Carol floated next to his sleeping cubby, staring down at a picture of a beautiful young woman she'd found while packing his personal items.

There was no name or date written on the back.

His wife? she wondered.

It made her feel sick with guilt that she hadn't even known if he was married.

Carol tucked the photo into the small container with the rest of his personal items. Then she closed her eyes and bid Sergeant Kenneth Miller a peaceful journey.

At the end of the long two days—after finally forcing herself to pack the personal belongings of Riley and Piper and store them alongside Miller's—she was presented with a close-up view of an uncharacteristically blue-tinted Venus. The traditional yellowish haze of the planet's atmosphere had been infused with swirls of blue. Lightning crackled in the murk.

Carol triggered the ship's automatic greeting protocol, sending out handshakes on every frequency and in every language.

What she got in return was a simple radar ping— an object in a high, precarious orbit around the planet, just now coming into view.

The magnified image on her control panel showed a small, dart-like ship: the *Seeker*. It wasn't in a tumble—which would have complicated any attempt at boarding or docking—but it did appear to be without power.

Carol began the tedious process of matching its orbit.

She swiped through the *Seeker*'s schematics on her control panel and found that she could directly dock the two ships. She released the *Odyssey*'s controls to the onboard computer to complete the final maneuvers.

With a gentle bump of airlock-on-airlock, the *Seeker* and the *Odyssey* met to form an X orbiting high above the stormclouds of Venus. The auto-locking seals engaged, securely connecting the ships.

Carol cycled the airlock and drifted into the *Seeker*.

The ship was dark. Ice crystals glimmered off every surface as light from Carol's helmet lamp swept the walls.

Three people in spacesuits floated in the cramped cockpit. Venus Lab's roster had listed three occupants: Sandra Jordan, Niels Erikson, and Hideo Tanaka.

Carol approached them hesitantly, her stomach sinking at the thought of what she might find.

All of them were alive—but only just.

Their wrist pads indicated they were breathing the dregs of their oxygen. The two men were unconscious, but Sandra's eyelids fluttered open when Carol pulled her toward the airlock.

"Jeff," she whispered.

"No, I'm Carol," said Commander Brighton.

"Find Jeff. He's still out there."

Carol opened her mouth to reply but quickly shut it again. If Jeff was outside the ship, that meant he had been EVA for forty-eight hours. Unless he had a pile of spare oxygen packs, there was no way he'd still be alive.

"Is he on Venus Lab?" asked Carol.

Sandra slowly shook her head. "It was destroyed."

Carol glanced at the other two men. "Let's get you into the other ship."

Two hours later, the *Odyssey* broke orbit and left the *Seeker* behind. Niels and Hideo had regained consciousness. Hideo rested in one of the sleeping cubbies, one arm draped over his eyes. Sandra sat in the copilot seat next to Carol in the command cabin, and Niels sat behind them.

"We're not leaving without Jeff," he reiterated for the tenth time.

Hideo spoke up loudly from the crew cabin. "He didn't have enough oxygen, Niels. I am sorry, my friend, but you're searching for a corpse."

"Doesn't matter!" Niels snapped. "We can't leave him out here."

Carol tapped on her control panel, plotting their course for Earth.

"I'm running every possible scan," she said. "Unless the ship finds him, there's nothing we can do. If his suit lost power..."

She didn't have the heart to finish the sentence. She had already delayed their departure by repeatedly scanning the same section of space, hoping for a radar blip.

But she *had* found the alien.

The sight of it froze her in place. The *Odyssey* had broken orbit, leaving the *Seeker* behind as Carol put some distance between her ship and Venus.

She watched with a mixture of awe and terror as the creature orbited the planet, traveling past her small viewing window. It was only the size of her finger at that distance, but Niels explained that it was much, much larger than the *Odyssey*.

"There might be a way to find Jeff," said Sandra.

She had been silent for an hour while Carol coaxed the ship's system through the best way to get back to Earth.

"I'm all ears," said Carol.

"Jeff said the torus that brought him back to Earth put something in his head," Sandra told her. "A small black sphere that lets him use fold space. I triggered the alien by broadcasting a signal at a specific frequency. If I use that frequency in a broader scan, we might be able to pinpoint Jeff's location."

"Assuming the sphere in his head responds to the frequency," said Niels.

Carol pulled up the broadcast interface on her control panel and gestured for Sandra to go for it.

She worked quickly, tapping out long sequences of numbers and manipulating an audio wavelength until it resembled a jagged mountain range.

"There," she said, tapping a final button to broadcast the frequency.

"That's it?" Carol asked. "How long will it take?"

Sandra shrugged inside her spacesuit. "Depends on how far away—"

BLEEP.

An external video feed popped up on the control panel. A pair of red brackets blinked around a gleaming object amidst a sea of stars.

Carol enlarged the image, focusing on the object between the brackets. The computer crunched the incoming video data, smoothing out a wall of blurry pixels.

The unmistakable shape of a spacesuit materialized in the blur, its face shield gleaming with reflected light from Venus.

Jeff Dolan drifted through space thirty miles from the *Odyssey*. He was in a gentle spin, his arms and legs unmoving.

"Let's pick him up," Carol said quietly.

They performed the duty with care, taking their time on approach to match Jeff's velocity. Carol still had an hour before she needed to start the first of the primary burns that would carry her new crew back to Earth.

Once the *Odyssey* was next to Jeff, traveling at the same speed, she opened the airlock. Using orbital thrusters on the side of the ship, she drifted toward him until the airlock swallowed him up.

A minute later, Carol and Hideo waited silently on the other side of the airlock until it pressurized.

Jeff bumped against the airlock wall and floated back toward the hatch. His face shield was cracked, obscuring his face.

Carol stabilized Jeff's spin while Hideo swapped out his failed power pack for a new one. The screen of his wristpad flashed red three times, then glowed green. A fan whirred within his oxygen pack.

Hideo frowned as he read data from Jeff's

wristpad. Carol watched him expectantly.

"He was out there too long," said Hideo. "Sixty hours with no oxygen. It's impossible that anyone could—"

Jeff's wristpad let out a single beep.

Carol and Hideo looked down at the screen.

Beep.

"What is that?" asked Carol.

"That," Hideo replied, "is a heartbeat."

32

JEFF

He awoke in a hospital room, sunlight spilling in through a large window. Dust particles danced in the light. A vase of colorful flowers occupied half the small table next to his bed. He was alone.

Jeff sat up slowly, with great effort. Every muscle in his body felt strained, as if they had been torn and sewn back together. His joints were stiff and swollen. Even the hospital bracelet on his left wrist hurt against his skin with the slightest movement. He eased back onto his pillow and looked out the window, not recognizing the city outside.

His gaze drifted to the call button on the wall next to his bed. He let out a slow sigh as he stared at it, too exhausted to lift his arm.

Some time later, the door to his room opened and a doctor came in. She wore a white coat over white scrubs, and bright pink sneakers. She made notes on her tablet and didn't look at Jeff until she was halfway to his bed. Then she stopped in her tracks with her mouth open. After a long moment, she smiled.

"You're finally awake," she said.

Jeff swallowed as he prepared to speak, but it felt like he was forcing broken glass down his throat. He nodded.

The doctor set her tablet down next to the flower vase and listened to Jeff's heartbeat with her stethoscope. With a quick nod, she slipped the stethoscope around her neck and began the process of checking his blood pressure.

Jeff looked at his hands while she worked. He slowly balled them into fists, then opened them. He didn't feel the same now as when he'd come back from Titan after his first mission. There had been no pain that time. He had felt like a new man. Now he felt as if he had been crushed and glued back together.

"I'm Dr. Cynthia Tate," said the doctor. "I've been looking after you since you arrived." She gave him a moment to respond, and when he didn't, she asked, "Can you speak?"

"Yes," he managed to croak.

Her smile grew wider and she picked up her tablet to scribble a note.

"How are you feeling?"

"Pain," he whispered.

"Where?"

He made a gesture to indicate his entire body.

"We can help with that," she told him. "I know from your x-rays that you have no broken bones. I guess that's your silver lining."

"Where..." he said, then stopped and closed his eyes against the pain.

"You're in Washington, D.C.," she said gently.

"You've been in a coma for two weeks." She watched him closely while she relayed the information. "Do you remember how you got here?"

Jeff tried to sit up, then quickly thought better of it and lay back onto his bed.

"No," he whispered. "Where's Kate?"

"I'm afraid I don't know who that is," said the doctor.

"No phone," he croaked.

"Pardon?"

He nodded toward his bedside table.

"There's no phone."

"This is the military ward. Sometimes they request no phones or TV. No one told me why you shouldn't have one."

"It's because he's supposed to be dead," said a gruff voice from the doorway.

Colonel Brighton walked into the room, frowning. His uniform had been immaculately pressed. His buttons gleamed and his black shoes reflected the room like mirrors. He removed his hat and tucked it under his arm, then ran a calloused palm over his buzzed hair.

"Getting phone calls from dead people tends to upset people," he said. "How is he, Dr. Tate?"

"Alive, but in pain."

"May I speak with him alone?"

"Of course," she said. Then she smiled at Jeff. "I'll get something to make you a little more comfortable."

He nodded his thanks as she left the room.

Brighton paced next to the bed, staring at Jeff as if he couldn't understand what he was seeing.

"I don't understand what I'm seeing," he said finally.

"Water," Jeff whispered.

"No, that's not it," Brighton replied, shaking his head.

"Water, please," Jeff repeated, pointing weakly at the sink next to the bathroom.

"Oh."

Brighton found a small paper cup and filled it. Jeff brought it to his lips with a shaking hand, but still managed to lean forward enough to get most of it into his mouth. He collapsed back down on the bed with a sigh, holding the empty cup on his stomach.

"Did she tell you how long you were in a coma?" Brighton asked.

Jeff nodded.

"On her way back to Earth in the Odyssey, my daughter picked up Niels Erikson, Hideo Tanaka, and Sandra Jones. They were adrift aboard your ship, the Seeker. They had no power and were almost out of oxygen." Brighton grunted. "That Erikson is a piece of work, but I have to give him some credit. Despite his eccentricities, he wouldn't allow Carol to leave until she either found you or confirmed you could not be found."

"Remind me to thank him later," Jeff said quietly.

Brighton looked at Jeff seriously.

"Dolan," he said. "Listen to me. The crew of Venus Lab were adrift for two days before Carol picked them up. It was another twelve hours before they found you."

Jeff met the Colonel's gaze and held it for a long time, waiting for him to say it was a joke.

He cleared his scratchy throat and whispered, "That's impossible."

"Lot of that going around," Brighton conceded. "Your body is sore because you were floating in open space for sixty hours...without oxygen."

Jeff shook his head. "Not possible."

But isn't it? he thought at the same time. *Who knows what the Worldshaper did to me?*

"You were dark purple when they peeled you out of your spacesuit on the Odyssey. They thought you were dead until they checked for a heartbeat. Three beats per minute, Dolan. So they piled on the insulating blankets and brought you back here." Brighton shook his head. "We thought it was unbelievable when the tori brought you and Riley back from the dead. But this...this is something else."

Someone entered the room, only this time it wasn't Dr. Cynthia Tate. It was a tall man in slacks and a button-down shirt. He smiled warmly at Jeff and gently shook his hand.

"This is Dr. Singh," said Colonel Brighton. "I asked him to come in here and explain the details."

"Good morning, Mr. Dolan," said the doctor. "We need to talk about something that might be a little difficult to grasp when you first hear it."

"Like surviving in deep space for more than two days?" Jeff asked.

"Which is a result of what we need to discuss, yes."

"What kind of doctor are you?"

"I'm a clinical psychologist."

"Uh oh."

Singh smiled again. "A sense of humor is a good thing. I think you'll be fine. We're in the 'managing expectations' phase of our conversation."

"By all means, proceed," Jeff whispered with mock formality.

"It's fortunate you weren't awake when they brought you here. I doubt you would have appreciated the, um, thoroughness with which the Colonel's doctors investigated your situation."

"That's not why I'm sore, is it?"

Dr. Singh chuckled. "No. You're sore because you were mostly dead for more than two days. What the doctors found after they ran all their tests on your blood, your tissue...after all the scans...is that your cells regenerate at an impossible speed."

"You should have been unrecognizable when they found you, Dolan," said Brighton. "Your soft tissue should have crystallized, including your organs. Yet your heart kept beating."

"The cellular regeneration anomaly is something the doctors really focused on," said Dr. Singh. "Not only because it fascinated them, but because of what it meant for you."

"What does it mean for me?" Jeff whispered.

"Well," said Dr. Singh. "If your cells continue to regenerate at this speed, you will never get cancer.

You may not even grow older. You're not going to die, Mr. Dolan. At least not from old age."

Jeff stared at the empty paper cup in his hand. He ran his thumb over the rim. Singh and Brighton watched him closely.

"Where's Kate?" he asked.

"She's here, in D.C.," Brighton replied.

"Does she know? About what you just told me?"

"She knows about the coma, but not the rest. I wanted to leave that decision to you."

Jeff absentmindedly bunched the thin hospital blanket in his hand and squeezing the fabric, his thoughts far away. "I think she'd catch on in about ten years or so."

Dr. Singh turned to the Colonel. "Please call me if anything changes."

"Thanks, Doc."

After Singh left, Brighton cleared his throat. "We have a lot more to discuss about what happened while you were near Venus. Kate can fill you in on some of it, and I can provide the missing pieces. I'd also like to know more about your interactions with the alien."

"Aliens," Jeff corrected him. "There was something on the surface...an AI, maybe. It said it wanted to test me."

Brighton raised an eyebrow. "To what end?"

Between pauses to rest his painful throat, Jeff paraphrased his conversations on Venus, attributing all of his experiences to the Worldshaper—he wasn't sure he wanted to tell anyone about meeting himself as the Envoy quite yet.

"It would remake Earth," Brighton mumbled, his jaw working. "Just like that? No negotiation, no chance to evacuate?"

"If it can't form a beneficial human connection, that's the impression it gave me."

"Beneficial. What does that mean?"

"As of right now, I have no idea."

"Do you think it could do such a thing? Is it capable?"

"From what I saw, it's more than capable."

"As if we're an ant hill meant for stomping," Brighton muttered under his breath.

"What about Riley?" Jeff asked.

The Colonel shook his head, no.

"Carol sent this from the Odyssey," he said, reaching into his pocket and pulling out a small tablet.

He showed Jeff the image on the screen. It was a blue firework in deep space.

"What is that?"

"The Earth-bound comet just before the Odyssey crew blew it to pieces." He slipped the small tablet back into his pocket. "They managed to knock it down from an Extinction Level Event to a meteor shower that hit half the globe. We'll be scraping up that blue gunk for years." He shook his head and looked out the window. "Who knows what it will do to the crops? The soil? We could be facing a global famine within four decades." He sighed wearily. "But that's for my successor to worry about."

"You're finally retiring?"

"I'll be available as an advisor, if they want me. Get some rest, Dolan," he added, not unkindly. "Dr. Tate knows how to get in touch with me when you're ready to go."

His shoes clacked on the hard floor as he left the room.

Jeff watched dust particles dancing in the sunlight over his bed and thought about floating in space, alone. He thought about his life with Kate. He thought about a distant future without her.

His gaze drifted down to his hands. When he looked up again, Kate was standing in the doorway of the hospital room, smiling, her eyes brimming with tears.

"Hey there, handsome," she said.

"Hey there, beautiful."

She sat on the side of his bed, and they hugged for what seemed like eternity.

EPILOGUE

Odyssey II — twice the size of its predecessor with three times the complement — waited in orbit around Venus for a month before the crew got the green light to move forward with their mission.

Commander Carol Brighton sat alone in the small viewing station just aft of the cockpit while Commander Timbwe, her copilot, conducted the final pre-mission briefing in the crew quarters midship.

Five years after Carol had returned to Earth on her previous mission, she was finally back in the black. Her father, the Colonel—now happily retired from his consulting contract with the United States Government—feigned surprise when she told him she was heading up the second Venus mission. Afterward, he smiled and said he'd expected her to take off sooner.

Carol had thought about signing on for a number of other missions in the interim, but that would have potentially sent her away when the crew of *Odyssey II* was chosen. Given the sensitive nature of the mission, she couldn't be left out.

She wanted to make sure it was done right.

The countdown timer on her console flashed zero. With a swipe of her finger, the view on her monitor shifted from the hazy yellow atmosphere of

Venus below—now with continent-sized gaps in the atmosphere from the alien terraforming operation on the surface—to an image of the horizon.

Carol drew a sharp breath as the alien creature in orbit appeared on the screen.

For five years it had waited above its intended home while its drones and machines worked to terraform the surface for habitation. For five years her military superiors on Earth had argued over the creature's fate.

Six months ago, the decision was made.

"They're not afraid it's a direct threat," her father had said after his last meeting with the officer who would replace him, "provided its connection with Jeff Dolan is enough to keep it away from Earth. The general consensus seems to be that it wouldn't be so bad to have a neighbor. Besides, the thing seems content to leave us alone and wait for Venus to change."

"Then what are they afraid of?" Carol asked.

"They're afraid Jeff Dolan will die and it will eventually turn its planet-changing technology toward Earth."

"Why does it want him in the first place?"

"Jeff says the connection is a bridge between our species, at least as far as he understands. It's supposedly how the alien will communicate with humanity if it ever needs to. But he hasn't heard a peep from it since returning from Venus, so who knows?"

Carol fidgeted nervously as the alien grew in size

on her viewscreen.

After the meteors fell five years ago, Earth's soil began to change. Most governments reported severe deficits in annual crop production. It was getting harder to farm. There was mention of famine.

Given that reality, Carol wasn't surprised to see military brass taking a proactive stance with the Venus situation.

She swiped through the sensor controls on her console and had the *Odyssey* run a full diagnostic of the creature. The results were the same as they had been since the ship arrived in orbit: no activity.

A major hurdle to taking any action against the alien was the simple fact that no one had any idea what it could do. Jeff Dolan's crew had witnessed some of it, but—after finally agreeing to be debriefed—even he couldn't be sure the alien wasn't hiding a trick or twelve up its sleeve. He told the brass everything to the limit of his knowledge, then gratefully returned to Cape Canaveral with Kate to build starship engines.

Then, a year ago, the creature went dormant.

It blinked out of all the scanners. Its energy signature snapped from lava-hot to glacier-cold in a heartbeat. The glowing red substance that filled deep valleys on its rock-like skin vanished.

The military decided it was time.

After the *Odyssey*'s last scan of the alien was complete, Carol sent the information back to Earth. She already had the operational go-ahead for the mission, but if something happened to her over the next few hours, she wanted her father to know she'd done her job.

Besides its size and number of crew, *Odyssey II* differed from its predecessor in another major way.

The ship had nine tensor net arrays bolted to the outside of its hull.

Carol had the computer double-check the equipment before deployment. She harbored her own private doubts about whether nine enormous nets would be enough to haul the creature back to the egg-shaped container Diamond Aerospace had unwittingly built for it in Earth's orbit. Five of the six orbital shipyards would indeed be used to build starships, but one of them—on perpetual lease to the U.S. government—would serve a very different purpose altogether.

People with more science degrees than her swore *Odyssey II* could handle the load—swore the nets would hold.

Beyond her immediate doubts, Carol couldn't stop asking herself what would happen *after* the mission. What if she succeeded in hauling the creature all the way back to Earth? What if it *did* sleep long enough to be stuffed into an orbital cage?

More importantly: what if it woke up?

She pressed the all-call button.

"Listen up, everyone. It's time. Get to your stations and keep your comms open. Let's go catch an alien."

KEEP READING for an exclusive excerpt from ANOTHER WORLD, the next chapter in the INFINITE SKY saga (or scan the code to learn more)!

More books by Samuel Best:

The INFINITE SKY Universe

Titan Chronicles

Mission One
Deep Black
Last Contact

Galena Chronicles

Another World
Third Colony
Galena

Pantheon

Forthcoming

You can find more info on the author's website
https://sam-best.com

About the Author

Born in Cape Canaveral, Florida, Samuel grew up a mile from the gates of Kennedy Space Center. His grandmother built space shuttles, his father designed scientific equipment that flew on them, and Samuel watched the launches from his rattling front porch, dreaming of the stars.

His best-selling novel Mission One, a near-future first contact odyssey, is the book that launched his career as a science fiction writer.

He recently spent three years traveling the world with his wife. They welcomed their son near the end of that journey and are now spending their days exploring the United States while Samuel works on his next book.

ANOTHER WORLD
400 years after the events of the Titan Chronicles

PROLOGUE

It was a wet, dirty morning, like all the rest of them.

The ticket man didn't care.

He whistled as he walked down a pedestrian lane, drumming his fingers against the large folded cardboard advertisement under his arm. Puddled sludgewater seeped into his tattered boots with every step. The intermittent oil-slick rain drizzle soaked his dark green jacket as water trickled down his back from a hole just under the collar.

Despite the dreariness, the ticket man's taut face twisted in a grin, revealing yellow teeth.

Above him, beyond the crumbling towers of downtown Houston, a pale, forgotten sun gleamed through a dense haze.

Ramshackle booths crowded each side of the narrow lane, some no more than a skeleton of pressed laminate planks connected by twine.

They advertised to the ticket man in faded, misspelled words, offering discounts on booze, smokes, and lottery tickets. Only a few were staffed. Their stalwart occupants were, without fail, toothless and weathered, clearly unable to afford even the most basic dermetic rejuvenatives. They grunted and turned away when they recognized the ticket man, waving him off dismissively.

Still, he didn't care. In less than a month, he would buy his Suncruiser yacht and sail away from the filth, into the Gulf and toward the golden horizon.

One month, he told himself.

The countdown had become his mantra, his lifeline. He'd made a promise to himself: no more scraping by. No more begging. He would escape, once and for all.

He would write his own destiny.

Naturally, escape required money. Where better to find it than with those who were also searching for a way out — or at least for a temporary escape from their sad reality?

The ticket man stopped in front of an empty booth. A few rain-soaked brochures lay in puddles, disintegrating on the pressed laminate counter, left behind by someone who had probably once held the same dream of escape clutched to their own malnourished heart.

He glanced up and down the lane. Seeing that no one was watching, he swept away the remnants of someone else's dream. With a flourish, he unfolded his cardboard advertisement and propped it on the counter. Gaudy colors exploded in fireworks behind plastic holding racks. Reaching into the inner pockets of his long jacket, he produced several thin stacks of glossy brochures and set them in the plastic holders.

He stepped back to admire the display.

See the World from Your Bed! promised one of the brochures, offering a near-impossible discount on the latest altered-reality body system.

Tickets to Sunrise Station — CHEAP! exclaimed another. Sled rides to the orbital station went for a premium price, but there were still a few bulk crates lying around in warehouses waiting to be discovered by those without black market qualms.

His best seller, though, showcased the simple silhouettes of a couple at sunset, overlooking a red canyon.

Find Love, read the brochure cover. Inside was a coupon for a one-night singles cruise over the city of Houston, booze included. The ticket man wasn't sure how the red canyon factored into it, but no one ever asked.

He wiped off a flimsy crate that had been kicked aside and sat on it.

There was no hurry. He only needed a few sales each week for the next month to buy his yacht. Through scrupulous planning and devious opportunism, he had tucked away enough money for retirement. To truly last in the business of sales, one constantly needed to unearth new ways of increasing one's profit margin — and the ticket man had been in the business a *very* long time.

Admittedly, it was getting harder and harder to dodge the authorities. A chronic indifference had plagued the local police until recently — an indifference which had allowed him and his ilk to thrive. Some recently-elected council member had undoubtedly lit a fire beneath them in order to stir up more votes for their next campaign, making the ticket man's job all the more difficult.

Perhaps that explains all the empty booths, he mused.

Back when he'd started hawking his wares in every avenue of greater Houston, this particular lane was bursting with activity. Tourists — such as they were in those days — could find anything the legal shops were unable to sell. This included not only items one would be ashamed to carry around in public, but harmless trinkets and everyday novelties that were banned for obscure reasons.

The ticket man listened to the gentle patter of rain on the ripped canvas roof of his temporary storefront.

The booth directly across the lane had been removed so a new billboard could be installed on the smeared wall behind. In a cartoonish, purposefully unrealistic style, it depicted a man in a robber's mask reaching for a young boy. The protective mother held on to her child with white-knuckled hands, recoiling in horror and screaming for the police. Bold lettering on the billboard proclaimed, *Stop Snatchers Before They Strike! It's YOUR Responsibility!*

The ticket man rarely reflected on his past, yet he never regretted not having children. Billboards like the one across from his booth only served as a reminder that he'd made the right choice. The minuscule amount of pity he occasionally conjured for his fellow humans was generally reserved for the adults who managed to bring offspring into the world.

He intended to ponder the subject in greater detail, but his reverie was interrupted when he heard a deep voice down the lane.

The ticket man leaned forward on his rickety crate to look. The lane was empty except for one man near the far end. He wore a loose plastic poncho and an oversized, misshapen backpack.

The booth occupant he spoke to pointed down the lane, toward the ticket man.

As the stranger approached, the ticket man leaned back in his booth well out of view. His eyes darted back and forth as he thought of every possible outcome, every possible escape route from the lane should the stranger turn out to be a policeman. By all the rules of law, the ticket man owned every ticket in his pocket, yet he hadn't come to own them in the traditional manner. A policeman surely wouldn't appreciate not being able to trace their origins.

The man in the poncho appeared before his booth, dripping wet from the rain. He looked up and down the lane, hesitating. He had the bearing of a strong man made weak by the vat-grown soy diet inflicted on the populace since Earth's soil had turned.

One month, thought the ticket man.

His jack-o-lantern grin split his face, and he asked, "A good, fine morning, innit?"

The ticket man laid out his offerings, conspicuously sliding the singles cruise brochure to the forefront.

"What are you searching for, friend?" he asked. "Eager to travel from your couch? Need to find a partner? No one should be alone."

The man in the poncho picked up the brochure offering a discounted ride to Sunrise Station.

"Ah," the ticket man said, nodding sagely as his potential customer flipped through the brochure.

"Looking to leave all of it behind. You know, I hear Sunrise has entire rooms dedicated to one type of food." The ticket man had heard no such thing. "Stuff you can't get here anymore. Fruits, vegetables, even meat proteins. They grow it up there, in space."

The man in the poncho tossed the brochure onto the counter.

"I need to go a little farther," he said in a low voice.

The ticket man studied him more closely. Square face, dark beard stubble, weary eyes full of suspicion, and clothes so shabby they made the ticket man's look as if he'd just plucked them off a store rack. The potential customer adjusted the straps of his over-sized backpack, hoisting the load higher on his shoulders. If the ticket man didn't know any better, he would have thought something inside had moved.

"No offense, friend," he said, "but you can't afford a ticket to the lunar colony. Everyone who can is already there, and the rest are at the end of that infamous hundred-year waiting list."

"I need to go farther than that."

The ticket man laughed. "But the only thing farther is—" He stopped laughing and sobered up in a snap. His eyes narrowed. "So you *do* have money. How'd you get it, I wonder?"

The man in the poncho offered no explanation. He stood still as a statue, dripping in the rain.

The ticket man shrugged nonchalantly. "What if I don't have the tickets?"

"Then I don't need you."

He started to walk away.

"Ho there, wait a minute!" said the ticket man, nearly falling off his crate. "Let's not jump to the end just yet. How many tickets do you need?"

The man turned back. "Just one."

"Why don't you buy it from the shuttle company?"

"I'm...traveling with someone."

"Ahhhh," said the ticket man as it all clicked together in his mind. "And you don't want them turning up on the official registry." He made a big show of scooping up the brochures on the counter and tucking them away in his jacket. "Well, look. I'd love to help you, but my operation is one-hundred-percent legal. I can't afford to be associated with black market sales."

He pretended to look for other customers, indicating the conversation was over.

"I can pay double," said the man in the poncho. He showed his credit card-sized hellocard, squeezing its worn metal grip reluctantly. The other half was a translucent screen, its orange glow flickering as rain spattered its surface.

The ticket man chewed on the proposition a moment. He reached into an inner jacket pocket and produced a card-reader cube, several inches to each side, worn and cracked. The screen on one side emitted a flickering orange glow, the same shade as the hellocard. He quickly tapped a long series of numbers on the screen and set the card-reader on the counter.

"Make it triple."

Enough to buy my yacht today, he thought.

The man in the poncho looked down at the glowing sequence of numbers on the small cube: 300,000. He stared at it for a long time. Just when the ticket man was going to pick it back up, the man in the poncho stepped forward and pressed the flat side of his hellocard to the screen.

The cube beeped, and the ticket man snatched it up greedily.

"My ticket," said the man in the poncho, leaning closer.

In no great hurry, the ticket man pulled out a black wallet from a zippered pocket in his jacket. He kept the contents hidden as he thumbed through the various rectangles of hard plastic. He found a stiff, transparent ticket with vibrant blue etchings, then read the name of the passenger as he held it out.

"Have a safe journey, Mr. Boone."

The man in the poncho took the ticket and walked away without looking back.

After he had turned the corner at the end of the narrow lane, the ticket man sprang to his feet. He whistled a cheerful song as he folded up his brochure-filled cardboard advertisement and tossed it behind the booth, then dramatically wiped his hands and kissed the whole mess goodbye.

As he strolled down the lane with his hands in his jacket pockets, rubbing one thumb over the screen of the card-reader, he made it a point to greet all of the other booth occupants — the bottom feeders who would still be there, soaking in the rain, fighting for scraps, while he lounged on the deck of his yacht that very evening.

He looked up at the tepid sky, grinning, and took a deep breath of polluted air.

What a sucker, he thought.

PART ONE: LEAVING EARTH

CHAPTER ONE

MERRITT

To enter Houston Spaceport, one first had to show proof of passage at the security gate. The gate was a series of stalls, each occupied by an employee whose sole responsibility was sifting wheat from chaff so that only verified passengers got past.

Merritt Alder stood in a light rain under a gloomy midday sky, watching those employees from under the dripping hood of his poncho. Between him and the gate, three security guards wearing full body-armor patrolled the entrance to the port, strolling slowly from one end of the stalls to the other. Each cradled a large rifle in their muscular arms. Black face shields under fitted helmets hid their faces.

Behind him, dilapidated skyscrapers shrugged in the rain, their broken windows sagging like sad eyes.

Merritt shouldered his heavy, awkward backpack higher and tightened the straps. His arms had gone numb an hour ago, but he knew it wouldn't be long until he could remove the load.

A wide tickerboard above the security stalls displayed a scrolling list of departure times for the bus and hyperrail depots — hundreds of them throughout the day — and a time for the next sled launch to Sunrise Station. If Merritt missed it, he wouldn't catch his connecting flight.

He swiped a finger over the cracked screen of his watch.

There was still time.

The concrete exterior of the spaceport vaulted up at an angle behind the tickerboard and disappeared into a thick haze. An orange glow bloomed deep within the mist: the burning engine of a sled as it launched into the sky, heading for Sunrise Station.

As the glow faded, a lone taxi rolled to a stop in front of the gate. A businesswoman in an expensive suit got out and hurried for the nearest security stall, waving her plastic, rectangular ticket at the employee.

The employee, an older gentleman with a face like stone, was unmoved by her demands for special treatment.

Merritt turned his attention toward the other stall employees.

He'd been watching them interact with passengers after they emerged from old, beat-up taxis. He'd been studying their mannerisms and their behavior patterns as they scanned ticket after ticket and answered the same questions again and again.

An older person would be ideal. Pensions were a thing of the past. Those beyond mandatory retirement age were always looking for a way to earn extra income. A small bribe could be enough to get Merritt through the gate without being interrogated. He had his hopes set on old stone-face in stall five, but after the back-and-forth with the businesswoman, he decided against it.

Eight of the ten other stalls were staffed by employees a decade younger than Merritt. He instinctively wanted to avoid bright-eyed overachievers — too much risk of them blowing their whistle for a chance at a commendation.

He needed someone halfway between hungry and indifferent — and if he couldn't get either of those, he'd have to settle for oblivious.

An elderly woman stood in the tenth stall, a permanent smile on her serene face. She waited for the next passenger with her bony fingers laced over her stomach. Most passengers went straight for the middle stalls, causing lines to form, but stalls one and ten were usually wide open. Either of those would allow for a modicum of privacy during the unavoidable conversation Merritt expected to endure.

He slowly walked toward stall number ten, pretending to be more interested in the empty street ahead of him than in the older woman.

There was a sharp *bwoop-BWOOP!* from behind. Merritt spun around to find the source, his heart thudding. An unmanned police cruiser rolled past, its blue-and-red lights flicking against the buildings on either side of the street.

"*Keep a hand on your wallets,*" said a robotic, monotonous voice from a loudspeaker on the roof of the cruiser. Bullet holes pocked the car's scratched and dented exterior. "*Mind your child. Don't let the snatchers get another one. Curfew is 10 PM. Be smart. Stay safe.*"

It disappeared into a heavy mist down the lonely street, its looped, endless warnings fading to eventual silence.

Merritt shook off the temporary fear and approached stall number ten. He presented two translucent rectangular tickets, each one etched with glowing blue lettering, but the old woman held up a finger for him to wait. A moment later, a young man entered the booth. He exchanged a few quick words with the older woman, then she left.

Merritt took a step back.

The young man's name tag read EDWARD. A black caterpillar mustache clung valiantly to his upper lip. He pulled on his headset and adjusted his seat, muttered something unflattering about the older woman, then crisply gestured for Merritt to approach the stall.

"Where you headed, poncho man?" he asked.

Merritt looked around, stunned with indecision.

"Yo!" said Edward. "What's the hold-up?"

One of the heavily-armed security guards strolled past, glancing in his direction. His hand moved noticeably closer to the grip of his rifle.

Merritt stepped toward the stall and slid his two tickets through the small slot at the bottom of the thick plexi window.

"Sunrise Station," he said.

Edward slid the tickets over a scanner built into the surface of his desktop. He typed rapidly on his keyboard. "Is that your final destination?"

He stopped typing and whistled as he read the screen, his eyebrows rising slowly. For the first time, he made eye contact with Merritt.

"You're going through the Rip? Well, lemme just get the red carpet ready for Mr. High Roller!" He chuckled, shaking his head. "Gonna leave Earth behind, is that it?" He smirked and typed on his keyboard. "I'm seeing one stop at Mars on your way out."

"That's fine."

"Is it? Great."

He stopped typing abruptly, then swiveled his chair around toward Merritt, a look of concern on his face.

"Two tickets," he said, holding them up. Then he pointed at Merritt. "Only one *you*."

Another security guard walked past the booth. Merritt waited until the guard was out of sight, then he carefully took off his unwieldy backpack and unzipped the top.

He held the opening toward Edward, who leaned forward uncertainly to look inside.

It was the second time he was surprised since Merritt approached his booth. He plopped back in his seat, rubbing his open mouth thoughtfully.

"You got guts," he said finally.

Merritt closed the backpack and pulled the straps up over his shoulders, grunting against the lopsided weight.

"May I pass?" he asked.

Edward sucked on his teeth while he mulled it over, tapping the plastic ticket against the palm of his hand.

"You know what?" he said, shaking the tickets at Merritt. "I'm gonna guess your real name isn't on either one of these. Do you know what that means?"

He held up a hand to call over one of the security guards.

Merritt stepped closer to the stall. "I can pay you fifty thousand."

Edward lowered his hand, the ghost of a victorious smile tugging at the edges of his mouth.

"Guy like you that can afford a trip through the Rip?" he said. "I think two-hundred K."

He set a card-reader cube against the plexi window with its glowing orange screen facing out.

"That's too much," Merritt said through clenched teeth. "That money is for housing and food."

Edward shrugged. "Suit yourself."

He beckoned one of the guards over.

"Two-hundred K," Merritt hissed.

Edward tapped the screen of the card-reader until the numbers read 200,000, then held it against the plexi, smiling smugly. Merritt glanced behind him at the approaching security guard. He hastily pressed the flat side of his hellocard against the plexi opposite the card-reader, swallowing the urge to vomit as the glowing numbers plunged lower on the screen of his hellocard and surged upward on the reader.

The security guard walked to the side of the booth. Edward stood and opened a narrow door, then spoke to the guard in hushed tones. They shared a laugh, then Edward nodded toward Merritt and rolled his eyes. The guard squeezed his rifle grip.

Merritt clenched his hellocard until it dug painfully into the flesh of his palm. He slowly turned away from the booth, preparing to run.

Edward slammed the door on the side of the stall and dropped back into his seat with a sigh.

"Okay, Mr..." he said, consulting the tickets. "Mr. *Boone*. Enzo here is the best guard in the force. The absolute *best*." Enzo made a rude gesture at Edward, who grinned without humor. "He's gonna escort you through security. Have a safe journey, blah blah blah."

He waved Merritt away from the booth indifferently.

Enzo flicked on his rifle safety and slung the weapon over his back. He walked through the security gate.

Merritt looked up at the sky, trying to see Sunrise Station through the haze. On a semi-clear day, which was the only good kind Houston experienced, it appeared as a small, gleaming metal asterisk arcing rapidly across the sky, its six tapered arms glinting as they rotated around a central core.

Part of him was happy he couldn't see it, for catching a glimpse of the station was one of the few truly beautiful reasons for remaining on Earth. As he followed the security guard through the gate, he hoped he would never see it from the surface again.

TULLIVER

The darkest moods find the darkest corners.

Tulliver Pruitt sat on an overturned suitcase in the shadows of a dusty room in a poorly-lit section of the Houston Spaceport, nursing one such mood. His thoughts were thunderous and grim, as they often were those days. The room had no door, and Tulliver sat in the dark, watching passengers scurry past without noticing him as they rushed to catch their rides.

He rubbed his thumb over a golden locket which lay open in his meaty palm. The slender gold chain dangled between his fingers. He stared down at the pictures of his wife and daughter, and he tried to cry.

Tulliver had never been able to conjure tears, not even when it concerned his family.

He snapped the locket shut and clenched it to his chest, taking a deep, cleansing breath, then rubbed his hand slowly over his bald head, wiping away the sweat.

Baggy clothes covered his loose skin. Tulliver was a powerfully-built man, over two meters tall, but he carried a lot of unnecessary weight. His shapeless clothes concealed everything but his sagging, jowly cheeks and the vague outline of a pear-shaped torso.

He wheezed.

Tulliver couldn't help it. He'd tried medication, tried losing weight. None were effective. His wife slept like a log, bless her, and never complained about his snoring. The problem was his nose. It was broad and squat, and difficult to breathe through, so Tulliver had to wheeze through his mouth.

On the floor next to him was a pile of forged tickets. One of them had enough travel credit left to get him through the first security checkpoint and no farther, but all of the others had been rejected by the self-scanners outside the sled terminal. Bright red lights flashed overhead whenever an invalid ticket was scanned, so Tulliver had decided to wait an hour between each attempt.

He tried the last ticket yesterday, so now he was stuck in limbo, unable to leave the terminal after passing through the first set of gates, and unable to pass through the next set without a ticket containing more travel credit.

Sleds launched to Sunrise Station several times a week, but only one more departure would get him there in time to catch his next ride. He needed to board that sled in less than two hours, but all he had was a pile of worthless tickets.

The silhouette of a man with shaggy hair stepped into view just outside the room.

"We got one, Tull," he said.

The gravelly voice belonged to Roland Day — a wiry, skeletal man half Tulliver's width and two heads shorter. Roland let his hair run shaggy to compensate for his inability to grow a beard — a sore point that one quickly learned to never bring up in casual conversation.

Tulliver carefully secured the locket in a zippered pocket of his ill-fitting, sand-colored jacket. He wheezed as he stood from the overturned suitcase, then left the pile of forged tickets behind as he followed Roland into the dim light of the starport.

Upon emerging from the muffled, cave-like room, Tulliver was immediately assaulted by sound and movement.

Tin music blared from unseen speakers. Video billboards covered every square inch of wall, shouting at him, selling to him, appealing to him.

One such billboard played a looping publicity reel for one of the two remaining pharmaceutical conglomerates. It showed a happy young couple cradling a newborn. The background was blown out, overexposed to imitate a brilliantly sunny day that no one believed in anymore.

"*Find out what the good doctors at PharmaGen are doing to fight Low Birthrate,*" proclaimed the billboard. "*Sign up for a local study today.*"

Tulliver followed Roland across a broad, open white concourse with a peaked ceiling reminiscent of a circus tent. Smeared, opaque windows shaped like teardrops let in a small amount of outside light.

Roland walked quickly, his shoes clacking loudly on the hard, polished floor. It didn't take Tulliver long to pick out his mark in the crowd.

A man in a tailored suit walked hurriedly across the room, heading for the sled terminal. One of his hands held a cup of coffee and pulled a small suitcase on wheels. With the other hand holding his phone to his ear, he struggled to keep the strap of his messenger bag from slipping down his shoulder.

A rectangular plastic ticket with glowing blue lettering bounced in his back pocket as he walked.

Roland glanced behind him, and Tulliver nodded. Roland sped up to a jog, passed the man in the tailored suit, then abruptly turned around and bumped into him. The man's coffee cup crumpled between them, spitting hot liquid everywhere.

While the man yelled his face red at Roland, Tulliver lightly lifted the ticket from his back pocket and whisked it into his jacket in the blink of an eye. Roland apologized a dozen more times before managing to extricate himself from the encounter, then met up with Tulliver around a corner.

"One more ticket to go," said Tulliver, holding up the hard piece of plastic. "After that, no more running."

Roland grinned and reached for it, but Tulliver snapped it away and wagged a finger at him.

"Uh-uh. You owe me for Dallas, remember?"

"That was six years ago!" said Roland, throwing up his hands.

"And I'm just about ready to forget about it."

He squeezed the back of Roland's neck and guided him toward the concourse to find a new mark.

"Oh, great," Roland growled as he looked across the room.

The man in the tailored suit was speaking to a group of armed security guards, excitedly pantomiming his encounter with Roland and the subsequent loss of his ticket.

The guards looked across the room in unison, and saw Roland.

"Time to go," said Tulliver.

He spun and bolted, his heavy boots and his heavy feet within them pounding the hard floor. Roland easily overtook him, running at full speed toward the last remaining automated ticket terminal.

He glanced back with wide eyes, his shaggy hair bouncing side to side. He slowed enough so he could reach out and grab for the ticket.

"Give it to me!" he shouted.

Tulliver shoved him away and looked back, wheezing hard. The guards were gaining fast. Just a few more seconds to the gate, but he wouldn't make it in time.

Roland could, if he had a ticket.

"Here!" shouted Tulliver.

Reluctantly, Roland slowed down as Tulliver held out his hand. Tulliver slowed down even more, hearing the boots of the guards right behind them.

"Come on, come on!" yelled Roland.

Tulliver grabbed something from his inside jacket pocket and shoved it into Roland's grasping hand, then stumbled into him, knocking them both to the floor. Tulliver landed on his shoulder and rolled away, screaming in pain.

"He has a blade! He has a blade!" he cried.

Roland sat on the floor, staring without understanding at the knife in his hand. Then he figured it out, and the confusion on his face turned to rage. He lunged for Tulliver, slashing with the knife, but the guards fell on him, slamming him to the floor.

As he screamed and fought, Tulliver shuffled away, holding his gut, pretending to be wounded. He fell against the automated terminal for support and swiped his stolen ticket across the screen. The plexi door slid open and he stumbled through, into a brighter section of the spaceport.

As the door closed behind him, one of the guards brought the butt of his rifle down to crack against Roland's head, silencing his squeals.

Tulliver straightened up and cracked his back. Giving one last look at the limp form of Roland as the guards dragged him away, he turned to find the boarding terminal for Sunrise Station.

LEERA

Leera bit nervously at one of her fingernails as she rode in the black limo on the way to the spaceport. Rain streaked the tinted back window, through which the blurred outline of her military escort SUV was barely visible.

Few drivers and even fewer pedestrians were willing to brave the storm. The empty streets and oppressive haze swirling overhead made Houston feel like a ghost town.

In direct contrast to the sterile uniform she endured at the lab, Leera now wore a short, black cotton jacket over a white T-shirt, with dark green pants and hiking boots. Somehow it felt more adventurous — more like she was going on safari instead of into the cold vacuum of space.

At fifty-five years old, she hadn't expected to do either.

The route to Galena opened when she was just a girl in Birmingham. Every child dreamed of going, but the earliest pioneers were unmanned probes. Humans wouldn't be allowed through the Rip until Leera was forty-seven. She figured by that time the opportunity to visit Galena would be awarded to any one of the dozen talented, fresh young graduates in her department.

That's why she was so surprised to get the contract.

Across from Leera, in the back of the limo, Paul leaned forward, smiling, and gently pulled her hand down into her lap. Her own smile was tinged with sadness as she squeezed his fingers tightly.

Ten years her junior, Paul hardly looked older than when she'd met him in his thirties. His short hair was putting up more of a fight than many of his peers, thinning slowly, but not receding. Like so many others, he'd received corrective eye surgery after it was lumped into the universal coverage initiative. Leera thought he looked even younger without his glasses.

Next to her, Micah sat leaning into her side, his hands on his thighs in proper fashion, staring out the back window. Leera's son rarely stopped running around long enough to show her any kind of affection, but he'd been a barnacle as of late. She wondered if he sensed she was leaving.

The boy had a keen sense of foreshadowing, picking up on signals to which Leera and Paul never gave a second thought: her empty travel bag pulled from a closet; a small container of toiletries; her adventurous attire, so different from her lab uniform.

Leera couldn't help but wonder if his prescience was a result of his condition — a heightened sense compensating for his losses.

Spinal meningitis had found him as an infant, permanently dulling his hearing, delaying his speech as a toddler, and causing recurring kidney problems.

The last round of treatments he endured resulted in a promising improvement, but he would soon need another to maintain his health. Leera planned to spend every last credit of her upcoming contract fee on a kidney transplant.

Her family had ridden in silence after the limo picked them up from their one-bedroom condo on the north side of the city. The entire morning had been silent.

Leera had known for almost a year she would be making the journey to Galena. Paul had known. They didn't have to talk about it for the first few months after her team had been approved for passage on the next tour. It hung quietly in the background, this enormous *thing*, pushed into the distance and safely ignored.

Micah was three. He would be five when Leera returned. So, yes, there were things to discuss. Many, many things.

Paul was handling the situation with his patented stoicism, attacking it from a practical angle. He broke her absence down into year-long chunks — 'bite-sized pieces', he called them. Two slender journals sat on his bedstand, each filled with scribbles of his plans with Micah while she was away.

He looked at his son, his brow knit with uncertainty. Leera was certain Paul felt more concern for Micah than he felt for her. Yet instead of bitterness, warm comfort washed over her, and she second-guessed her decision to leave for the nth time.

The limo stopped in front of the spaceport's employee entrance. Leera picked her travel bag off the floor and set it in her lap. She gripped the handle nervously.

"Are you coming in?" she asked.

"In this weather?" Paul replied, craning his neck to look up at the sky. "Of course."

She couldn't help but smile. "I told you to stop being so charming, or I'll never leave."

"That's not really motivation for me to stop, is it?"

The driver came around and opened their door.

"Ready, bud?" Paul asked loudly as he picked up Micah. "It's wet and cold."

He ducked out into the rain and hurried for the spaceport. The port was a towering concrete monstrosity, the shape and size of which one had to stand ten blocks away to fully grasp.

Leera ran after them, her hiking boots splashing in puddles, until they stood under an awning out of the rain. Micah leaned his head on Paul's shoulder and grinned.

"Was that fun?" asked Leera.

He nodded.

Four armed soldiers got out of the escort SUV and walked unhurriedly through the rain.

"Dr. James," said one of them in a booming voice, "if you and your family will follow me, we'll get you through security."

He spoke quietly to the other three soldiers. They fanned out behind Leera and her family as they entered the building.

The lead soldier swiped his badge on a keypad by the employee entrance, and the heavy metal door slid open.

Leera clutched her bag to her side with one hand and held Paul's hand with the other. Micah clung to his father's neck as they walked through the spaceport.

People stared, but Leera couldn't be sure if it was because of the military escort, or because of Micah.

"I saw another news story about a missing child at the port," said Paul as they walked. "He was taken *after* his parents got him through the security gates. Those snatchers are getting bolder."

"Fewer children to go around," Leera replied. "More people willing to pay for them." She squeezed Paul's hand. "I spoke to the Board of Directors. You'll keep the military escort until I get back."

"It's been nice taking him to the park," he replied, nodding toward Micah.

Leera brushed a strand of brown hair away from her son's face. He had her hair, straight and thick, though his was not yet lined with silver. He had his father's pug nose. She tapped it and he smiled.

They reached an automated ticket terminal and stopped. The soldiers stood a respectful distance away, and Leera realized this was it — this was where she left her family.

Paul set Micah gently on the ground and took his wife's hands. Leera found she couldn't meet his eyes.

"It's two years," she said quietly.

"Two *short* years."

He wrapped his arms around her and held her close. When she tilted her head up to kiss him, there were tear-marks on his shirt.

She knelt and put her hand to Micah's cheek. He looked down at the floor.

"I love you very much," she whispered, unable to speak louder. "Mommy will be back before you know it."

She hugged him fiercely, choking back a sob, then kissed his forehead and stood.

"I love you," she said to Paul, then she swiped her blue ticket at the terminal and went through the gate.

"*Don't look back, don't look back,*" she muttered as she walked away.

She turned around. Paul and Micah were already being guided back through the spaceport by the soldiers. She watched until they disappeared from sight, then reluctantly shouldered her bag and continued on.

The main sled terminal was a large, circular room with a low ceiling and a thick, concrete central pillar. Sedate food stands and coffee trolleys hugged the pillar. Four boarding gates lined the outer circumference of the terminal, each crowded by twenty or so ratty, upholstered chairs. Most waiting passengers leaned against a wall or sat on the floor.

Leera stood at the entrance to the circular terminal, unsure which gate was hers. She checked her ticket, but could find no gate number.

"Dr. James?" a man said behind her.

She turned and saw bright red hair. It belonged to a short man in a dark blue suit. He had a small mustache the same coppery red as his cropped hair, freckled cheeks, green eyes, and pale skin.

They shook hands. He spoke very quickly, in a thick, Scottish accent, and said, "Glad to finally meet ya. I'm your liaison for the tour. If you'll come this way, the other team members are already here."

Leera followed him to an unmarked door between two gates. He held it open and gestured inside, raising his bushy red eyebrows apologetically.

"I know it's not so fancy," he said. "Better than outside, though, eh?"

Leera walked into a small meeting room with dirty walls. A dim, buzzing fluorescent overhead light illuminated a warped card table, around which sat the other two members of her team and a young man with a shaved head in a Marine Corps field uniform.

She sat in the last empty folding chair next to Walter Lyden, the team's physician. In proper Walter fashion, he wore the same attire as he did at the lab: one of his several blue puffer vests over a long-sleeved, gray thermal shirt, and thick cargo pants. Most of the course hair atop his head had migrated south and settled in his red beard. He was one of the few who hadn't gone in for corrective eye surgery. He adjusted his thin spectacles and spun a Styrofoam coffee cup in his hand, looking at Leera as if to say, *What have you gotten us into?*

She shrugged, then arched an eyebrow at Walter's cup, intrigued by the prospect of coffee. Walter made a disgusted face and quickly shook his head, warning her off.

Next to him sat Niku Tedani, the team's microbiologist. His straight black hair was pulled back in a ponytail. He sat with his arms crossed over a light blue, collared shirt. A slight smile graced his broad, smooth face, as if he was privately amused by the current situation.

"Right," said the liaison, shutting the door behind him. He stood at the head of the table and clapped his hands once, then spoke in a clipped, rapid manner. "You three brainiacs are familiar with each other. We've got a medical man, a microbiologist, and a systems biologist," he said, pointing at Walter, Niku, then Leera. "This is Corporal Miles Turner." He motioned toward the marine. Turner nodded at each of the others. "I'm Kellan McEwan, your government liaison. Some of you know a little, some of you know even less. We've got a lot to go over and only twenty-five minutes to get through it before you board the sled for Sunrise Station. Now that we're all best friends, let's get started."

He withdrew a palm-sized, shiny black disc from his pocket and set it on the rickety table.

"Galena," he said.

A thin blue beam of light extended from the center of the black disc, then expanded into a flickering, glowing blue-green sphere two feet above the table.

"Only habitable world we can find that side of the Rip," Kellan continued. "Perfect ratio of land mass to oceans, as you can see. It was named for the abundant mineral lead sulfide deposits on the surface, which are visible from orbit. You can see a patch there," he said, pointing at a small gray smudge of dirty silver hiding in the green.

Leera found herself mesmerized by the hologram. She had never seen a rendition of Galena in such great detail. The planet spun slowly. It was covered in a maze of narrow, green land formations that seemed to crawl like snakes through bright blue oceans. Two large continents on opposing sides of the planet formed misshapen blobs, each roughly the size of Australia.

"Gravity is a comfortable ninety-nine percent of Earth's," Kellan went on. "You can't tell the difference."

He tapped the middle of the black disc and the hologram vanished.

Leera and the other three around the table leaned back in their squeaky chairs, blinking off their collective trance.

"Look," said Kellan. "I know that none of you wanted to get in bed with the government. I can't blame you. It's not like we have the best track record lately. I wouldn't be here if your grants hadn't fallen through. But they did. So here we are. Right then. Moving on."

He stuck his hands in his pockets and paced the room as he spoke.

"Cygnus Corporation is a third-party company which owns and operates the starliner that will carry you through the Rip and on to Galena. They are contracted by the government for that purpose. We can't afford to build our own, so we have to use theirs. It allows us to run scans on the surface, measure the weather, all the technical stuff we can get out of the way without actually going to the surface. The company makes extra cash by taking tourists through the Rip. It's good for everyone. Each trip, they've been sending down colony supplies, things like house kits and crop silos. If we weren't forced to delay the initiative so long, the colony would already be thriving. But no one has been allowed on the surface of Galena. Until now. You'll be traveling with the first wave of settlers. It won't be many, I'm sad to say. Most canceled their contracts when Cygnus started charging an arm and a leg for the journey. Those who are still going are farmers and pioneers who will lay the groundwork of our first extrasolar colony. While *you* are only contracted for a two-year tour, many of those you're with will make Galena their permanent home. They'll be stockpiling food while trying to adapt Earth crops to the foreign soil so we won't have to choke down that spliced-soy garbage we grow in plastic tubes. But the food will be too heavy to send back to Earth. That's not a practical choice, which is why we need to move there."

The room was achingly silent for a long moment, then Kellan continued.

"Now, you're probably wondering why we're having this meeting in the first place after all the hoops you had to jump through to get your contract approved. Well, you've been given clearance to wander the countryside, so to speak. You'll run your tests, collect your samples, do your research. Who knows? Maybe you'll even get to name something after a loved one. It's a new world, after all. Corporal Turner will make sure you go about your business undisturbed."

"We weren't told there would be a military escort," said Leera.

"Surprise," Kellan replied with a wry smile. "The truth is we don't know everything that's down there. But I can tell you that our scans have shown no significant lifeforms."

"*'Significant'*?" said Niku.

"Nothing larger than a teddy bear." He held up a warning finger. "Except in the oceans. We've detected *massive* movement below the surface, but our scans can't make out any details. Could be organic, could be land mass. Either way, best not go for a swim."

Leera, Niku, and Walter shared a hesitant glance.

"Everybody good with what we've covered so far?" Kellan asked, his arms spread as if he welcomed comments or questions. "Yes? Good. Okay. Now we come to the heart of it. Running this kind of operation isn't cheap. The contract with Cygnus Corporation expires after your return, and they're asking far too much money for a renewal. The people I beg for funding are going to say no. That means you might be the first and last scientific expedition to Galena. It *also* means the colony will die before it has a chance to take root."

He paused dramatically so his audience could absorb the information.

Leera chewed her lip nervously. She had no idea the fate of future travel to Galena was balanced on a knife's edge.

"Look at our planet," Kellan said gravely. "No livestock. No crops. Birthrate is dropping faster than we can reproduce. Earth is done with us. We've tried to fix it, but nothing is working. Galena is our chance at a fresh start, but the people in charge need a reason to keep going back, something they can use to justify the expense. Simply starting another colony is not it. I'm not alone in my belief that this is the right course of action, but my allies bear the heavy weight of bureaucracy. Those people don't deal in hopes and dreams. They need more tangible currency. A native plant that boosts fertility. A sapling that will spawn entire forests so we can have trees again. You're all here because you're the best in your respective fields. Whatever the reason to keep going back through the Rip, you have to find it. Otherwise we lose Galena. Because this is how we leave Earth. This is how humanity survives."

"What if we don't find anything?" asked Walter.

"I really hope you do," Kellan replied. "Your fee for this tour depends on it."

They stared at him, dumbfounded.

"You didn't read your contracts?" he asked incredulously, looking at each of them in turn.

"Why put it in the contract at all?" asked Niku.

"Retrieving such a sample is absolutely *vital* to our future," Kellan answered, jabbing the tabletop with his finger for emphasis. "We need to make sure the people we send have a reason to succeed beyond their innate curiosity."

Leera shifted in her uncomfortable chair. Without that extra money, there would be no more treatments for Micah, no more medicine.

"So, run your tests," said Kellan. "Learn what you can about the planet. But, I beg you, bring something back that will change their minds."

Kellan stood up straight and took a deep breath.

"Okay," he said. "Speech is over. Sorry. I get a bit carried away sometimes."

"You convinced *me*," said Walter.

"Well, that's a start." Kellan pulled three translucent tickets with glowing red lettering out of his pocket and set them on the table. "Here are your red tickets. Swap them out for your blues before you leave. Trust me, you'll appreciate it on the ship." He looked each of them in the eye. "Good luck out there."

Kellan walked out of the room quickly, leaving silence in his wake. Corporal Turner stood, saluted the scientists sharply, then followed after him.

Leera picked up a red ticket and thoughtfully turned it over in her hand.

"What do you think?" asked Niku.

Leera sighed. "I think we have our work cut out for us."

Grab your copy of *Another World* by scanning the code below or visiting
https://mybook.to/galenachronicles

Printed in Great Britain
by Amazon

30823613R00175